Carole, Lisa, and Stevie finished up the last of their chores and then escaped to the hayloft for a quick Saddle Club meeting. The hayloft was one of their favorite places. It was filled with the sounds and smells of the stable but was above the hubbub of activities.

"The show's going to be so much fun," said Lisa.

"Yeah, it'll be great watching Veronica get beaten in every class," Stevie said. "We're going to have to leave early." Getting up in the morning was not her favorite thing.

"And get here early," said Carole, thinking about the long drive into town at dawn to get on the road just two days after Christmas.

"I've got an idea," said Lisa. "Why don't we stay here the night before? That way we'll know Stevie will get up on time, we can make sure the horses are properly prepared for the trip, *and* we'll have more fun together."

"Count me in," Stevie said.

"Me too!" Carole agreed.

"It's beginning to feel a lot like Christ-mas!" Stevie sang, off-key.

ᵗʰᵉ SADDLE CLUB

BEST FRIENDS

BONNIE BRYANT

A SKYLARK BOOK
NEW YORK • TORONTO • LONDON • SYDNEY • AUCKLAND

RL 3.6, AGES 008–012

BEST FRIENDS
A Bantam Skylark Book / November 2001

ISBN: 0-553-48743-4

Published simultaneously in the United States and Canada

Bantam Skylark is an imprint of Random House Children's Books.
SKYLARK BOOK, BANTAM BOOKS, and the rooster colophon are
registered trademarks of Random House, Inc. Bantam Books, 1540
Broadway, New York, New York 10036.

PRINTED IN THE UNITED STATES OF AMERICA
OPM   10 9 8 7 6 5 4 3 2 1

For my best friends—every one of you.

Bonnie Bryant

"IF I SEE one more flake of snow this winter, I'm going to scream!" Stevie Lake declared, practically screaming even as she said it.

"Oh, come on, Stevie," Carole Hanson, one of her two best friends, responded. "That's not reasonable. It's only the middle of December. And remember, we want to have snow for the Starlight Ride on Christmas Eve."

"That's the point," Stevie said, fiddling with the napkin dispenser on the table. "We've already had three snowstorms. This is just going to be one of those winters, and I don't like it. Everything gets cold and mucky. We never get enough snow to play in or to close school, just enough to make a mess."

1

"Hear! Hear!" their friend Lisa Atwood chimed in. "It's been pretty awful. We've been confined to riding in the indoor ring since the beginning of November."

And that, of course, was what really mattered.

Although the three girls were very different from one another, their common love of horses drew them together. Once they'd discovered the possibilities of a friendship based on that love, they'd formed The Saddle Club. It was a simple organization with only two rules: Members had to be horse-crazy (easy), and they had to help each other out, no matter what (not always so easy).

Carole was the horse-craziest of the three. It seemed to her friends that her whole world centered on horses, and Carole would never have disagreed. Her room was covered with pictures of horses; her bookshelves were filled with books about them; her magazine collection was all about them. Carole wasn't sure what she wanted to be when she grew up—a competitive rider, a trainer, a breeder, a veterinarian, an instructor, or just an owner. Most of the time, she thought she ought to be all of these things.

Carole could be forgetful about many things. Sometimes her socks didn't match, sometimes she left her book bag or her lunch at home. But she never forgot to bring her riding clothes on days she had lessons, and she never forgot to bring a treat for her horse, Starlight. Her father, a colonel in the Marines, had bought Starlight for her one Christmas with the money her mother had left for her when she'd died.

Lisa was as organized about everything as Carole was about horses. Her clothes were always neatly pressed, her hair always combed smooth. Her assignments were never late and the only grade she ever seemed to get was an A. Her parents had just separated, and she lived with her mother. Her father was living in an apartment nearby, and she saw him every other weekend. Everything seemed different, and different didn't feel very good. It was especially hard now that they were about to have their first Christmas as a split family.

If Lisa was organized about everything, Stevie was organized about nothing. Her clothes were often wrinkled, rescued from the laundry pile that she called her closet floor. She was often late, she sometimes forgot assignments, and she was frequently distracted by her compulsion to play practical jokes, especially retaliatory ones, on any one or all of her three brothers. Stevie spent a good deal of time in hot water with one authority figure (parent) or another (school administrator). She sometimes had difficulty seeing what she'd done wrong, but she was awfully grateful to her friends, whose devotion and skills helped her get out of trouble almost as often as she got into it.

The waitress arrived at their table. Tastee Delight, or TD's for short, was one of their favorite places, and the girls were treating themselves to some ice cream before their afternoon ride.

"Oh, it's you," their waitress said, looking warily at Stevie. Stevie was famous—perhaps even infamous—at TD's for her odd ice cream combinations. The waitress was not always enthusiastic about her choices.

"Strawberry," Stevie said. "In a dish."

"And?" the woman asked expectantly, obviously waiting for Stevie to order licorice bits, caramel sauce, or pistachio ice cream to go with it.

Stevie fumbled in her pocket and pulled out the handful of change she had to work with. "Just strawberry," she said. The waitress sighed gratefully.

Carole and Lisa placed their orders and the waitress disappeared.

"Well, it's almost Christmas," Stevie said. "I've got to save up, even though I was tempted by the bubble gum syrup."

Lisa and Carole exchanged glances. "I think we can consider this our Christmas present," said Carole. "I mean, not having to watch you eat a crazy concoction."

"You could be right," Stevie said. "But I don't even have time to worry about money now. There's so much to do!"

"You bet there is," said Lisa. "All that Christmas stuff, especially the Starlight Ride, and then the horse show."

"Right," said Carole. "The Carolina Invitational. Did you ever think we'd be asked to go?"

They hadn't thought it would be possible. The Carolina Invitational was a very exclusive show that allowed only a limited number of riders to apply. Max Regnery, their riding instructor, had been invited to send four junior competitors. Much to their delight, he'd chosen all three of them. Less pleasing was that he'd also chosen Veronica diAngelo.

Veronica was their least favorite rider at Pine Hollow: She was about as annoying as anyone could be. For one thing, she never let anyone forget that her parents were very wealthy. If she couldn't earn something, she could always buy it—or at least she thought she could. Also, she considered Red O'Malley, Pine Hollow's chief stable hand, to be her personal servant. And perhaps the most annoying thing of all—and even The Saddle Club couldn't deny it— was that she was a pretty good rider. She wasn't as good as she thought she was, but she was good, and that rankled them no end.

"Well, there's lot to be done for just the show on its own," Lisa said. "Like filling out the application."

"You haven't sent it in yet?" Carole asked. That surprised her, since Lisa was usually so organized.

"Not yet, but the deadline isn't for a while. At least I've got it."

"Me too," Stevie said. "I wrote away for it the day I heard we could go, and I sent it in yesterday."

"I sent mine last week," said Carole.

One of the things the girls had learned early was that every show had its own rules and regulations. For the Carolina Invitational, which they were now referring to as the CI, the only deadline was for requesting the application. The riders could submit it up until a week before the show. They wouldn't have to pay the entrance fee until they registered at the show.

"I applied to be in a couple of jump classes," Carole said. That didn't surprise her friends. Carole was great at jumping, and Starlight seemed to have been born for the sport.

"Well, you'll do great, especially now that you've got that awesome new bridle for Starlight. He's going to love it and jump like a pro—as if he didn't always jump like a pro. It's dressage for me," said Stevie. "The CI is famous for its dressage tests."

Although all aspects of riding in competitions required discipline, dressage was the one that required the most. The rider and horse were required to proceed through a predetermined course of movements, turns, gait changes, reverses, and patterns, and it all had to look completely effortless. Many riders thought of dressage as the most demanding of events. Stevie, whose strong suit was rarely discipline in any form, took to dressage as if it were the most natural form of riding.

"Well, I'm applying for an intermediate jump class and dressage, but I also want to do a pleasure riding class," Lisa chimed in.

"Sounds good to me," said Carole. "You'll learn a lot from all of them. The best thing about shows, really, is learning. Some people think the purpose is to gather blue ribbons, but the only person worthy to compete with is yourself, as you know—"

"Hold it, Carole," Stevie said, smiling. "We know this stuff, remember? It's Veronica who needs that lecture!"

Carole smiled in response. "Right. Sorry," she said. She knew a lot about horses, and she was always happy to share. The problem was that her sharing sometimes turned into a lecture. Stevie had once told her that she was inclined to give twenty-five-cent answers to nickel questions. In this case, she hadn't even been asked anything!

Fortunately their ice cream arrived and they could change the subject to *Mmms*.

Stevie took two bites and realized something was

missing. "This needs a cherry," she said. "And maybe some whipped cream. They don't charge for that stuff, do they?"

"I don't think so," said Lisa. "You could ask."

Stevie picked up her dish and went to the counter to negotiate an upgrade on her ice cream.

"Stevie always knows how to get the most for the least," Lisa remarked, admiring her friend's powers of persuasion.

Carole winced.

"What's up?" Lisa asked.

"Oh, I don't know," said Carole.

"Carole!" Lisa said, genuinely concerned.

"Well, I didn't want to upset Stevie. She's going to do wonderfully at the CI, but I've got a problem. It's Starlight's new bridle," said Carole.

"Starlight seemed just fine with it," Lisa told her, confused.

"He is fine with it, but I had to spend every last penny I had on it. Now I don't know if I'm going to be able to pay the entry fee for the CI!"

"Maybe you shouldn't have bought the new one—" Lisa protested.

"Like I could ride in a show with a bridle held together by duct tape?" Carole reminded her.

"Oh, right, that," said Lisa.

"And even the duct tape was getting worn out."

"I remember," Lisa told her. "Look, I'm sure things will

work out. It'll be all right. I bet you'll get some money for Christmas."

"Not that much," said Carole. "And Dad has told me tons of times that since he pays Starlight's board and vet bills, all the other expenses are on me. I know that's fair. Right now, though, it doesn't feel fair."

"You *can't* not ride in the show," said Lisa. "For one thing, it won't be any fun if you're not there. For another, you're the best rider of all of us, the most likely to bring home blue ribbons. Um, not that that's what counts. . . . On the other hand, blue's a nice color."

That made Carole smile. "You're right. Something will work out."

Stevie returned triumphantly, bearing a dish of newly adorned strawberry ice cream.

"How'd you do it?" Carole asked.

"I convinced the guy behind the counter that strawberry sauce on strawberry ice cream is really an extension of the ice cream itself and so it isn't really a sundae. Once he'd bought into that idea, the chocolate sauce and the marshmallow fluff were a breeze!"

Halfway through Lisa's own sundae, her pager went off. It was her mother calling.

"I'll be right back," she said. "Don't anybody touch my ice cream."

Stevie looked at Lisa's very ordinary hot fudge on vanilla—no nuts, no whipped cream, no cherry. "No problem," she assured her friend.

"So, when do you get the dressage test?" Carole asked. Competitors received the test they'd have to perform before the show so that they could memorize and practice it.

"I don't know," Stevie said. "And to tell you the truth, I really don't even know if I can go."

"Why not?" Carole asked, surprised to find Stevie in her own boat.

"It's my new boots," she said.

"You don't have new boots," Carole reminded her.

"I know," said Stevie. "But I have to have new boots. My old boots don't fit me anymore."

"Want to borrow my old ones?" Carole asked.

"Wouldn't do any good," said Stevie. "I've grown two boot sizes, and that makes my feet *three* sizes bigger than yours. So I can either compete barefoot, or . . . well, you get the picture."

"Oh no," said Carole. "What about Christmas money?"

"You mean the eight dollars I've saved up to buy presents for my brothers and my parents?"

"Well, that, too," said Carole. "I meant, what if you get money from family for Christmas?"

"Unfortunately I'm not related to Fort Knox," said Stevie. "The boots and the show each cost about seventy-five dollars. I have enough money set aside in my special horse account for one but not the other." She dropped her voice to a whisper. "Here comes Lisa. I don't want to tell her. She's still upset about her parents' split; she doesn't need anything else to worry about."

Carole felt a twinge. She should have thought of that before she emptied her problem on Lisa. "Don't worry," she said. "I won't say a thing. You shouldn't worry, either. Something will work out. I'm sure."

"I hope so," said Stevie.

Just then one of the other Pine Hollow riders came over to their table. It was Joe Novick. He was licking the remains of an ice cream cone off his fingers.

"Can I ask you something, Carole?"

"Sure," she said.

"I've been having trouble with Calypso," he said. "It's like she's getting lazy."

"I noticed," Carole said. "She's taking those short little steps all the time."

"Any suggestions?"

Stevie hid her smile. That was the sort of question Carole loved. Did she have a suggestion? She had several.

The first was to work Calypso on a longe line, and when she got good with that, Joe should add some cavalletti.

"If you space them properly—and that's a matter of fine judgment . . ."

Forty-five minutes. That's how long Stevie was sure Carole could and would go on with Joe.

"Why don't you *show* him what you mean?" Stevie suggested.

Carole nodded. "Good idea. Come on," she said. Without pause, she put some money on the table to cover her ice cream and took Joe by the arm. They were out the door before Joe knew what had happened.

Stevie thought it was great that Carole had helpful answers for Joe. She just didn't want to listen to them right then. She returned her attention to her sundae and waited for Lisa to come back from the phone.

When she returned, Lisa looked quizzically at Carole's empty seat.

"Joe Novick needed to know about longeing and cavalletti," Stevie said. Lisa needed no further explanation. She knew exactly where Carole would be when they went to Pine Hollow for their lesson.

"Isn't it wonderful to have a friend who knows so much?" Lisa asked.

"Absolutely," Stevie agreed. "But sometimes I would

rather eat ice cream than hear about proper ways of spacing cavalletti."

"Me too," said Lisa.

"Your mom okay?" Stevie asked.

"Yeah, but she wanted me to know that she'd be working late today. It seems like she wants every extra minute of work she can get. She's worried about money all the time." Lisa paused. She looked unhappy, and Stevie wasn't surprised. Lisa's parents' separation was hard on her—even though she tried not to show it. Lisa swallowed. Stevie waited, wondering what was on her mind. "You know, Stevie," she began, "I hate the idea of asking her for money to enter the CI. It's so expensive!"

"I know," Stevie said, dismayed for Lisa. Worrying about her parents was one thing, but it wasn't any fun to worry about money on top of that.

"Ever since Dad left, it's been difficult for Mom. And Dad, too."

"And you?" Stevie asked.

Lisa sighed. "I guess," she admitted. "Not that it would be a hardship for me to skip the show, but . . ."

"Don't worry," Stevie said, recalling Carole's words to her. "Something will work out."

Lisa smiled. Something *would* work out. She just didn't see how it was going to be something good.

"I didn't want to say anything in front of Carole," she said. "I don't want to complain to her about my mom and dad. After all, I've still got two parents."

"Something will work out," Stevie repeated reassuringly.

"Sure," Lisa said, but she wasn't sure at all. "We should probably get over to Pine Hollow before Joe suffocates under the ton of information Carole's loading on him."

It seemed like a good idea to Stevie. They paid and headed out the door, following their friend to the stable.

2

"IT'S OKAY, CAROLE, I've got the idea," Joe was saying as Lisa and Stevie approached Pine Hollow's indoor ring.

"Well, the angle of Calypso's hoof should be—"

"I know. She has to lift it properly, right?"

"He needs help," Lisa said to Stevie, recognizing a person who was filled to the bursting point with Carole's knowledge.

"Oh, Carole! There you are!" Stevie called.

Carole looked up. She had been concentrating so deeply on the angle of Calypso's hooves going over the cavalletti that she seemed almost surprised to see her friends at the stable.

"Yes?"

"Time to tack up Starlight for class," Lisa told her.

Carole looked at her watch. When it came to horses—especially her own—she was all business. "We'll finish this later," she said to Joe.

There was a genuine look of fright on Joe's face. "There's—there's more?" he stammered.

"I'm sure by now Joe's got the idea of what he needs to do," said Stevie.

Joe waved to her gratefully as she and Lisa ushered Carole into the stable.

The first person they saw was Veronica, strutting along the aisle, as far from her own horse's stall as she could be.

"Shouldn't you be tacking up Danny?" Stevie asked.

"I don't want to hover while Red is doing his job," she explained.

"Might break a nail," Lisa said sarcastically.

That made Veronica look at her nails. They were perfectly polished, as always. The rest of Veronica was just as spiffy as her nails. She was always immaculately, and expensively, turned out. Her riding coat was tailored and her stock pin was eighteen-karat gold. Even a simple riding class was an opportunity for Veronica diAngelo to show off.

"You see," Veronica said, "I need to concentrate on rid-

16

ing skills, not stable skills. That's how I'll take all the blues at the CI."

"Speaking of which . . . ," a familiar voice interrupted. It was Max. He had a way of knowing everything and being everywhere at once. "You all have received and submitted your applications, right? And class begins in ten minutes. Remember, this is a special class I'm holding for the four of you on your show skills, so be prepared to do your best, as always. Stevie, make sure your reins are smooth this time. Carole, you can't lean so far forward over the jump the way you did in the last class. Lisa, I don't want to see your legs flapping. And Veronica, the judges are more interested in your skills than in your clothes."

Their heads spun as he walked away.

"Do we ever do anything right?" Lisa asked.

"Some of us do," said Veronica, making Lisa wish she hadn't asked the question.

"Well, at least we've all got our applications," Carole said.

Lisa and Stevie nodded. Veronica paled.

"You have requested it, haven't you?" Carole asked. There wasn't much time left before the deadline.

"Of course I have," she said. "I'm sure I told Daddy's secretary to do it about a week ago. She must have done it."

Veronica slid away, clearly not wanting to discuss the subject any further.

"I think Daddy's secretary is about to get a piece of Veronica's mind," said Lisa.

"If she gives away too many pieces, she won't have any mind left," Stevie observed.

Lisa laughed.

"I doubt that Daddy's secretary is working today anyway, because it's Sunday," said Carole.

"I'm surprised Veronica doesn't hire someone to compete for her," Lisa remarked. Her friends agreed.

TEN MINUTES LATER Max called the class to order. Stevie was the last to arrive, but she was lined up and ready to go just in the nick of time.

He began with limbering exercises for the riders and horses, having them circle the ring first at a walk, then at a trot, and then, when the horses were loose and relaxed, at a canter. He slowed them down and had them change gaits and directions several times. Then it was time for the real work to begin.

It turned out that, for The Saddle Club, the best part of the class was the warm-up, because it was the only time they weren't making terrible mistakes.

They began with a short jump course. Carole went first.

There were five jumps set up in a simple X pattern. *Nothing to it*, Carole thought as she entered the ring. She circled once, then she and Starlight went over all five jumps smoothly, keeping an even gait and sailing easily over each one. At the end she pulled to a halt in front of Max. She was sure she hadn't been leaning too far forward and that Max would be as pleased as she was with her performance.

"Disqualified," he said.

"What?"

"You forgot to tip your hat to the judge before you began," he told her.

Carole's heart sank. What a dumb mistake! She couldn't believe she'd done that—or rather *not* done it.

She walked her horse back to where the other riders were waiting.

"Tough," said Stevie.

"You'll remember when it counts," said Lisa.

"My turn," said Veronica. She did not forget to salute the judge. She and Danny did a fine job going over the jumps.

"Nice," said Max.

Stevie and Belle ticked one of the jumps as they went over. That would be enough to cost her a ribbon in the real competition.

When it was Lisa's turn, Prancer kept speeding up and

slowing down. In a real competition, that would put her at the bottom of the class.

Things didn't get better for The Saddle Club when they moved on to dressage. Stevie got totally turned around and did the entire test backward. That earned her the word *disqualified* from Max as well. Carole and Lisa managed to do the test in the proper order and direction, but they didn't do it very well.

The look on Veronica's face when she took to the course was one of total triumph. And Max's word for her performance was, once again, *Nice*. That was high praise, coming from him.

Stevie's heart sank.

They didn't do well in the pleasure class, either. For some reason Prancer got it into her mind that she really wanted to take things at her own pace, and Lisa had a hard time getting her to follow directions. Max couldn't keep from frowning. This, which should have been an easy practice for both Stevie and Carole, turned into a difficult one when Starlight became sluggish and wouldn't change gaits when Carole told him to. For Belle it was a whole different issue. She changed gaits every time she heard Max give the word. That was all well and good, except that it was clear to Max, as it would have been to a judge, that Stevie hadn't yet given the aids for the gait changes. Max frowned at her, just before he told Veronica she'd done a nice job.

At the end of the class, Max spoke to them all.

"Look, sometimes practicing for a show can be difficult," he began. "And making mistakes is part of it. If you don't make mistakes when you're practicing, you don't know what you should be practicing and you'll make all your mistakes in the show."

It was supposed to be a comforting speech, but Carole didn't find any comfort in it. "He said the same thing to the five-year-old beginner class before the D-level Pony Club schooling show last month," she told Stevie and Lisa.

"I wonder if there are any openings in that show," Lisa said. "I'm sure it's the one I should be entering."

"Let's try not to get down on ourselves," Carole said. "I think all of us need to do some more work. Back in the ring, girls!"

Lisa couldn't have agreed more, though at the moment the idea of getting back in the ring didn't hold much charm. Still, she settled resolutely into her saddle. Maybe this time she could do something, *anything*, right.

"Going out to torture your horses some more?" Veronica asked as she handed Danny's reins to Red. She received three glares for her trouble.

The next half hour did nothing to dispel any of The Saddle Club's gloom. Things had gone badly during class, but they went worse afterward. Carole fell off Starlight going over an eighteen-inch jump. Stevie was baffled when Belle balked at a lead change as if she were facing a five-foot jump, and Lisa got her diagonals mixed up at the trot.

"Here's the good news," Stevie said when they finally gave up for the afternoon. Carole and Lisa looked at her expectantly. It didn't seem to them that there had been much good news at all that day. "We're creative," Stevie informed her friends. "See, we never make the same mistakes twice. We're so smart, we keep finding new and different ways to mess up!"

"I don't think there's a ribbon for that," Lisa said. She pulled Prancer to a halt outside the stable door and dismounted. It felt like the first thing she'd done right all day.

"Well, as far as I'm concerned, the good news is that I've got a science project I have to work on this afternoon," Carole said. "It has to be finished before school closes for the holidays, and I'm sure to do a better job on that than I have with Starlight today."

"And I need to get home," Lisa said. "My mom seemed kind of down, and I want to make her a nice dinner."

"At least you two have something to look forward to," Stevie teased. "I have to go to the mall—"

"What's so bad about that?" Lisa asked.

"—with my brothers," Stevie said, completing her sentence. "Our Christmas present for our parents is going to be a portrait of the four of us. Going to the mall isn't hard. Smiling when I'm surrounded by my brothers . . . well, that's a challenge!"

Lisa and Carole laughed. Stevie and her brothers had more fun fighting than smiling together, but the girls suspected they'd all manage.

3

STEVIE DIDN'T JUST dislike cold weather, she *hated* it! She pulled her scarf tight around her neck and yanked her hat down over her ears. Walking to school instead of taking the bus didn't improve her mood.

What did improve her mood was spotting Lisa as she neared her friend's house. The freezing walk would definitely be improved by some good company.

"Morning!" she greeted her friend.

Lisa pulled the door closed behind her and waved to Stevie, who had stopped to wait for her.

The two of them went to different schools. Stevie and her brothers attended Fenton Hall, a private school, while Lisa, like Carole, went to Willow Creek Junior High. Even though they weren't going to the same place, they were at least headed in the same direction.

"You miss the bus again?" Lisa asked.

Stevie shrugged. "But the good news is that my brothers caught it, so at least I don't have to travel with them!" Neither of their schools was far from where Stevie and Lisa lived, and even though Stevie was walking, she would still probably get to school on time.

"How'd it go last night?" Lisa asked. When Stevie didn't respond, she continued, "At the mall. With your brothers."

"I knew what you were asking," Stevie said. "I was just trying to figure out how to describe it."

"That bad?"

"No, actually, that good," Stevie said. "For once, none of my brothers was a total pain. We kind of had fun and the photographer was a riot. I think it's going to be a great picture. Mom and Dad always love it when we do things that show how much we love one another—you know, like pretending it makes me happy I've got these awful brothers— so I know they're going to love the picture. The best part is that we put a deposit on the picture a long time ago, so none of us had to pay much for it last night, and the fact that I don't have any more money for Christmas is probably okay."

"That's good," Lisa said.

Stevie cringed. How could she be so insensitive? There she was, yammering about her brothers and her parents, and Lisa's parents had just split up and she was going to have to cope with a difficult Christmas.

"I'm sorry, Lisa," Stevie said. "I didn't mean to hurt your feelings. It's just . . ."

"Oh, no," Lisa said. "You didn't."

"But with your parents splitting and all, I should have . . . well, you know."

"I know, but don't worry about it. That's my family. You've got yours. Doesn't mean I don't envy you sometimes."

"You mean you want my brothers? I could have them packed up by this afternoon!" Stevie teased, trying to lighten the mood.

"No, it's not that," Lisa said. "I am upset about my parents splitting up, but that doesn't have anything to do with your family. Don't sweat it, okay? I don't want you or Carole to treat me any differently than you ever have just because everything else in my life is changing. At least *that* should stay the same!"

"Deal," said Stevie, and she resumed her chatter about the photographer. "So Michael kept doing this thing where he would grimace instead of smile and the photographer

26

would ask him what was wrong and he told the guy that I was pinching him. I wasn't! I wasn't even close enough. So then they all started arguing. It turned out that Chad and Alex were pinching him, not me. Are you sure you don't want at least one of them?"

Lisa laughed. "No thanks, you can keep them!" she said.

"While I was at the mall, I left the boys at the video store long enough to get to the tack shop. They had these beautiful boots—"

"Stevie!"

"They're a creamy dark brown, not black, with a rich, deep shine."

"You sound like Veronica," Lisa teased.

"And I'm about to sound more like her," Stevie said. "Because I bought them."

"Really?"

"I had to have new boots," Stevie told her. "My other ones are way too small. The last time we had a schooling show, I could barely walk for a week afterward."

"I remember," said Lisa.

"And these were on sale. They're even a little big for me, which means I can wear them now with extra socks and they'll still fit when my feet grow another size."

"So how beautiful are they?" Lisa asked.

27

"The most," Stevie assured her. "In fact, I'm thinking I should get a new helmet—one of those sort of dusky brown ones—to coordinate with my boots."

"Now you *really* sound like Veronica," said Lisa, laughing.

Stevie paused and glanced at her watch. They were approaching Fenton Hall, but she still had a few minutes and she knew Lisa would be on time. Lisa was always on time for everything, even when she seemed to be running late. Stevie tugged her scarf back up around her neck. Something was bothering her and she'd withstand a bit more of the cold to get to the bottom of it.

"Listen, there's something I want to ask you," Stevie said.

"Sure," Lisa responded.

"Carole seemed a little upset yesterday, more than she should have been about messing up at the practice. Do you have any idea what's going on?"

Lisa sighed. "I'm so glad you asked," she said.

"Why?"

"She didn't want me to tell you, but you've asked and that's not the same thing as just telling, is it?"

"Not at all. What is it?"

"You know Starlight's bridle?"

"The one that's all shiny with duct tape or the brand-new gorgeous one?"

"Both, I guess," Lisa said. "Anyway, Carole told me

28

that she spent every penny she had on the new bridle. There isn't anything left, like for the registration fee for the CI."

"You can't mean she's thinking about skipping the show!" Stevie said.

"She's thinking she doesn't have any choice," said Lisa.

Stevie hefted her book bag off her shoulder and dropped it on the ground with a groan of frustration.

"I told her something would work out," Lisa said hastily, and Stevie knew she was trying to comfort her as well.

"Something," Stevie said. "Look, I've got to go."

"Me too," said Lisa. "See you later." She hurried off to the junior high school two blocks away.

Stevie picked up her book bag and slung it onto her shoulder. Carole not compete? At the CI? In jumping? She almost couldn't imagine it. Carole and Starlight were a great jumping team.

There must be *something* she could do.

THAT'S ODD, THOUGHT Lisa, glancing around the cafeteria. Carole was sitting at a table in the corner. Because they were in different grades, she and Carole had lunch at different times, but there was her friend, munching on a carrot.

Lisa bought a salad, a container of juice, and a cup of yogurt and went over to her friend.

"Hey, what are you doing here?" she asked, sliding into the seat across the table from Carole.

"Eating lunch," Carole said. "I had to spend last period with my science teacher working on my project."

"Oh, right. Well, this is my day to run into friends," she said, opening the yogurt container. "I walked to school with Stevie."

"She missed the bus again?"

"Yep," said Lisa. "But she got there on time anyway. I think."

"After yesterday's practice, it's a wonder that any of us can do anything right," Carole quipped.

Lisa suspected that meant all had not gone well with the science project.

"Stevie was full of stories about how much fun she'd had with her brothers at the mall last night. She's sure her parents are going to love the picture."

"Anytime she has fun—or can admit she's having fun—with her brothers, it's got to be a special occasion," Carole said, smiling.

Lisa told Carole about the pinching incident and Carole laughed, easily imagining the event.

"That poor photographer!"

"The best thing is that she found a gorgeous pair of boots.

She sounded like Veronica when she was describing them, using words like *creamy* and *sheen*."

Carole's eyes lit up. Anytime one of her friends found something good for riding, it was enough to make her happy, too.

"Oh, Stevie really needed those," she said. "Her old ones were hopeless."

"I remember," Lisa said. "And she said they were on sale."

"You mean she *bought* them?" Carole asked.

"That's what I said, didn't I?"

"No. You said she'd found them. I didn't realize she'd paid for them. Is that what she did?"

"I think that's the customary way to buy," Lisa told her.

"She can't afford them," said Carole.

"They were on sale," Lisa reminded her.

"But Stevie needs that money for her CI entry fee. She told me she couldn't do both. I thought maybe she could borrow boots from someone."

"Oh no!" Lisa exclaimed.

Carole glanced at her empty tray. "I've got to get to art class," she said, standing up. "I'll see you later, okay?"

Carole picked up her tray and headed for the door. She paused, then turned back. "Hey," she said. "Don't tell her I told you."

"Sure," Lisa agreed.

Lisa took a bite of her salad and recalled her conversation with Stevie. She'd seemed so pleased about the boots and she hadn't said anything about the CI being a problem for her. Sure, she couldn't compete in the boots that were too small, but now that she had the new ones, she might not be able to compete at all. Something had to be done, and fast! Lisa just didn't know what.

STEVIE BROUGHT THE wheelbarrow to the door of Barq's open stall so that Carole could pitch a forkful of manure into it. The two of them were taking care of some barn chores while Max worked with Lisa on her pleasure class skills.

"Lisa's practicing really hard," Carole said, glancing out the stable door into the outdoor ring, where Lisa and Max were working with cavalletti. It was a difficult drill for both horse and rider.

"I think she always finds it easier to concentrate when she's upset," said Stevie.

"She's upset?" Carole asked.

"Oh, I think I hurt her feelings today, even though she said I didn't," Stevie said. "I kept going on and on about me and my brothers at the mall last night, and then I realized I was being just a touch insensitive to someone whose family is breaking up."

Carole picked up another forkful of soiled straw and aimed it at the wheelbarrow.

"I think Lisa knows the difference between your family and hers," said Carole.

"That's what she told me," Stevie said. "She also told me that you and I should keep treating her exactly the same as we always have."

"It's not easy when everything's changing for her."

"Just what she said," Stevie said. "She's a good sport, you know?"

"I know," said Carole.

"You don't know *how* good," Stevie said.

"What do you mean?" Carole asked suspiciously.

"Well, since you asked . . . ," Stevie began, recalling Lisa's rationale for sharing information with her earlier that day.

"I asked," Carole said firmly.

"She told me she's really worried about her mom and dad in lots of ways, and one of them is money. Like, all of a sudden, there are two households and a lot of new expenses. Her mom is working extra hours. She told me she didn't think she'd be able to ask them to pay for the CI."

"You mean she might not go?"

"She might not be *able* to go," Stevie corrected her. "But Christmas is coming. Maybe she'll get some money from some of her aunts and uncles or something."

33

"Right," said Carole. "Christmas can be great that way." She spread some fresh straw on the floor of the stall, her mind racing much faster than her pitchfork. Lisa was a relatively new rider, but she was good and she was learning very fast. A show like CI was just what she'd need to make it to the next level.

Carole looked out the door again: Lisa in the saddle, totally focused on the task at hand. That kind of work should be rewarded.

But how?

"GOOD, STEVIE, GOOD. Keep it up, now. Stop moving your knees. Shorten the reins. Good, good, now to the right and pick up a trot."

Lisa and Carole watched Max work with Stevie.

"She's doing something right," Lisa said excitedly.

"Unlike yesterday," Carole agreed. They were both very relieved to see things going better today, though it would have been difficult for things to be any worse than they had been the day before.

"You did well with the cavalletti," Carole said.

"I hate those drills," said Lisa.

Max had laid the cavalletti—which were long poles—on the ground at specific distances to control the length of

Prancer's stride. After fifteen minutes of that, Prancer's gaits were smoother and Lisa's control was greater. "It's just boring."

"Yeah, but it works," Carole said, pleased with the fact that both Lisa and Stevie were doing much better at their show skills.

When it was her turn, Carole was much more successful at jumping than she had been the day before.

"Nice, Carole," Max said.

Carole beamed.

When they'd finished their special show lesson, Max asked the girls to cool down their horses, groom them, and water them. "Then come to my office," he said. "There are a lot of details we have to discuss."

Carole's feeling of well-being disappeared. There were a lot of details about any show, but in the case of this particular show, it seemed there was only one detail that mattered: She had no idea how she was going to pay for it. As Stevie had pointed out, though, perhaps the answer would appear under the Christmas tree. She sighed. It was going to take a lot more loving relatives than she had to solve this problem.

The girls settled into chairs in Max's office, waiting while he shuffled through papers. Like Carole, Max was totally organized when it came to horses but sometimes a little bit less than organized in other respects, like with paperwork. He moved one big pile, grimaced when he saw what was under it, and quickly replaced it.

Fortunately, Mrs. Reg appeared in the doorway, ready to lend a hand. She was Max's mother, widow of the former owner of the stable. She was the stable manager and, clearly, the organized one in the family.

"Looking for this?" she asked, handing him a file folder neatly labeled CI.

"I was wondering where you'd put it," Max said sternly, taking it from Mrs. Reg. The girls stifled giggles. He was trying to sound annoyed, but everyone there knew he was relieved by his mother's organizational skills.

"Okay, here's what's going to happen," he said. "I'm giving a couple of clinics at the CI grounds two days after Christmas, but the competition doesn't begin until two days after that. Deborah and I will leave the day after Christmas and fly down with Maxi." Deborah was his wife, and Maxi was their daughter. "Mrs. Reg will stay here, and she'll be in charge while I'm gone.

"We've got four riders and horses coming to the CI," he continued, consulting the file. "You girls will ride down with Red in the trailer. It's a long ride, and it'll only tire everyone out if you try to do it in less than two days. I've called a friend in North Carolina who will let

37

you stay in his barn overnight, so plan to bring sleeping bags."

"Food?" Stevie asked.

"Of course, we'll take all the grain and hay we need for the show. It's a good idea to have the horses remain on familiar food when they're competing hard."

Carole nodded in obvious agreement.

"Not for the *horses*," Stevie said. "For us!"

"Bring everything as if you were going camping," said Mrs. Reg.

"It's not like this travel stuff is the hardest part," Carole said.

"Well, it's often the most complicated," Mrs. Reg said. "Competing is usually the easiest part of a show."

"Maybe," said Carole.

Lisa cringed when she heard Carole say that. Mrs. Reg had no way of knowing what was really on Carole's mind, and it wasn't Lisa's place to tell her.

"None of this is made easier by the fact that it's the middle of winter," said Max.

"But that's why it's an indoor competition," said Stevie.

"And it should be warmer in South Carolina than it is here," said Lisa.

"Oh, don't worry, any of you," Mrs. Reg said. "It's all

going to work out. And the good news is that the show takes over the grounds of a school, so you can all stay in the dorms for no charge."

"Dorms?"

Stevie didn't have to turn around to see who had asked that question. The voice was all too familiar. Only Veronica diAngelo could utter a word with such complete disdain.

"Yes, dorms," said Mrs. Reg. "They offer housing to all competitors and participants, including grooms and equipment managers."

"That's nothing, Veronica," Stevie said. "We're going to get to sleep in a barn on our way there."

"That's what you think," said Veronica. "Do you really think I intend to sleep with animals?" She looked around at Stevie, Lisa, and Carole, making it obvious that she considered them animals as well. Stevie couldn't help glaring at Veronica.

"I think the Four Seasons is fully booked," Max said, teasing her.

For an instant Veronica looked horrified. Then she relaxed.

"It's not, actually. Daddy's secretary made reservations for my mother and me there. It's about ten miles from the show, but we're renting a car anyway, so it'll be easy to get back and forth. We're flying there the day after Christmas, so I'll be acclimated."

"You're expecting jet lag on a one-hour plane trip?" Lisa asked.

"In the same time zone?" Stevie added.

Veronica did not dignify their questions with an answer.

"So the only thing left is to be sure that Danny will arrive on time—and in good condition." She spoke the last words heavily.

"I'm sure you can count on your friends to see to that," Max said, looking at The Saddle Club.

"I'd never let anything bad happen to a horse," Carole said. It was true and everyone knew it. No matter how much Carole disliked Veronica—and on a scale of one to ten, it was an eleven—she'd never take that out on her horse.

Veronica was apparently counting on that. "I'm sure," she said. "Well, then, it's settled. Now I need an equipment manager. Max, can you recommend anyone?"

The girls cringed. Max expected his riders to look after their own equipment during a show. He couldn't stop a rider from hiring an equipment manager, but he liked to think that his students were capable of looking after all aspects of their own horses at all times. He also knew that they were all capable of pitching in and helping one another—all of them except perhaps Veronica.

"I'm sure you'll manage fine on your own," Max said.

"Well, I'll tell you it's going to be a lot harder to focus on winning ribbons if I have to spend all my time worrying about whether my saddle is properly polished."

Max ignored her last comment and excused the riders from his office. He told Veronica he'd meet her in the ring in five minutes for her lesson, so she'd better hurry and get Danny tacked up. She left his office, calling, "Red!" Red, of course, was the one who was going to have to hurry and get Danny tacked up.

Stevie, Carole, and Lisa filed out of the office. Carole hadn't finished putting away her tack before they'd started their meeting, and her friends followed her to Starlight's stall, where she'd left her bridle and saddle on a sawhorse.

Veronica stood in the aisle nearby, watching Red tack up Danny.

"Funny thing," said Stevie.

"What's that?" Lisa asked.

"I never realized Veronica could be concerned about whether her saddle was polished. It never seems to bother her here."

"Maybe it's the jet lag," said Lisa. "Brings on that kind of worry." The girls stifled giggles, aware that Veronica was trying to ignore them.

"Come on," said Carole. "Let's get out of here." She picked up her tack and turned to leave.

"Nice bridle!" said Veronica.

The words surprised Carole.

"What?" she asked.

"I said, that's a nice bridle." She pointed to the one that Carole was holding—the new one. "But I miss the old one. It was so colorful and sparkly. What was that, duct tape?"

Carole could feel her cheeks redden. It was so like Veronica to be unaware that horses cost money and that not everybody had as much of it as Veronica's parents did.

"It was a good bridle," Carole said defensively.

"It must have been," Veronica told her sweetly. "Otherwise, why would you have kept on using it way past its natural lifetime?"

That was as much as Carole wanted to take.

"I've kept it, you know," Carole said.

"Whatever for?" Veronica asked.

"As a reminder of how lucky I am to have this new one, and of how good the new one is," Carole said.

Veronica was clearly working on a retort when Red came to everyone's rescue.

"He's ready," he said, leading Danny out of the stall. "And I think you'd better hurry because Max is ready, too." He pointed to the ring, where Max was waiting impatiently.

Veronica left them without further comment.

"Thanks," said Carole.

Red shrugged. "Veronica's Veronica," he said.

The girls finished up the last of their chores and then escaped to the hayloft for a quick Saddle Club meeting. The hayloft was one of their favorite places. It was filled with the sounds and smells of the stable but was above the hubbub of activities.

They settled on bales of hay.

"The show's going to be so much fun," said Lisa.

"Yeah, it'll be great watching Veronica get beaten in every class," Stevie said. "We're going to have to leave early." Getting up in the morning was not her favorite thing.

"And get here early," said Carole, thinking about the long drive into town at dawn to get on the road just two days after Christmas.

"I've got an idea," said Lisa.

Carole and Stevie looked at her.

"Why don't we stay here the night before? That way we'll know Stevie will get up on time, we can make sure the horses are properly prepared for the trip, *and* we'll have more fun together."

"Count me in," Stevie said.

"Me too!" Carole agreed.

"And the best part is that since Veronica is leaving the day after Christmas, we won't see her for three full days!" said Stevie.

"We won't miss her one teeny-tiny bit," said Lisa.

"It's beginning to feel a lot like Christ-mas!" Stevie sang, off-key.

LISA FINISHED THE last of her math homework, double-checked her answers, and then put the page aside in her finished-homework folder. Her history questions were already there, as was her French vocabulary exercise. She always felt so satisfied when her homework was both finished and well done. There were things in life over which she had no control, but homework was not one of them.

She pushed back her chair and reached for her copy of *Gone With the Wind*. It was a great book, and she was loving it—even more than she'd loved the movie. There were some papers under the book.

Her heart sank. It was the application for the CI. She'd sent away for it the very first day Max had told them all to do it, and she'd gotten it back right away, but she'd had a hard time filling it out. As little as three months ago, she wouldn't have given it a second thought. She would have filled it out and then told her parents how much money she needed. They would have given her the cash and she would have put it in an envelope to take with her to the show so that she could pay when she registered.

Nothing was that simple anymore. Her mother was working extra hours, and her father always looked drawn and tired when she saw him.

It wasn't that the Atwoods were ever that rich, but nobody in the family had really worried about money before. At least it had seemed that way to Lisa. Now it seemed that everything was about money. Lisa's mother had said she couldn't get her a new outfit for the holidays this year because "money's tight." Lisa didn't need a new outfit for the holidays. She had plenty of clothes to wear, but her mother had always had fun buying her new ones. Even her father, who had never complained about money, had mentioned to Lisa that he'd seen an apartment he'd wanted to rent, but he'd chosen a less expensive one instead.

Lisa picked up her book and settled onto her bed, where the light for reading was just right. She didn't open the book, though. She lay back and let her mind wander.

It was just a few months ago that her parents split up.

Until that day, Lisa had thought everything was just fine. But it wasn't. Things must have been going wrong for a long time and she'd never noticed. It made her wonder how much else she hadn't seen. She was just about to tell herself that this kind of self-pity wasn't going to get her anywhere when there was a knock at the door.

"Come in," she said.

Mrs. Atwood entered and sat on the edge of Lisa's bed.

They talked for a few minutes about Lisa's homework and school in general. It seemed funny to Lisa that the thing she'd always been the very best at, schoolwork, was something her parents never seemed to notice when they were together. Now that they were separated and planning a divorce, they asked about it all the time. Lisa wasn't sure they cared about it any more than they had in the past, but asking about homework sometimes made it possible to keep from talking about things nobody wanted to talk about.

"All done," Lisa said. "I'm going to read for a little while now before I turn out my light." She tapped the book on her lap.

"I loved that book," her mother said. "But don't read too late."

"Promise," said Lisa. She smiled a little bit inside. She was almost always good about going to sleep at a reasonable hour, and her mother knew it.

"Listen, I had an idea," her mother said. Lisa waited for her to continue. "There's an exhibition of impressionist paintings at a museum in the city. I have to work on Saturday, but I was wondering if you'd like to go with me on Sunday afternoon. That way you could go riding with your friends in the morning, and then we could have lunch and go to the museum in the afternoon. I mean, if you'd like."

"I'd like," Lisa said.

"Good." Her mother smiled and then gave her a goodnight kiss before she left the room.

Just a few months earlier, whenever Lisa's mother wanted to spend time with her it seemed she wanted to be at the mall. Lisa liked having nice clothes, but she'd never been bitten by the shopping bug quite the way her mother had, and it was never much fun for her. Impressionist paintings would be much better.

She picked up her book, but before she could begin to settle into antebellum Atlanta, the phone rang.

"Hi, sweetie." It was her dad.

"Hi, Dad."

"Am I interrupting something important, like homework?" he asked.

Lisa smiled. *Two for two.* "Nope, it's all done. I'm just reading. And then I'm going to sleep."

"Good day?"

Lisa thought about it for a second. "Good day," she said. "I had a riding lesson, and for once I didn't mess everything up!"

Her dad laughed. "That definitely qualifies as a good day. There are a couple of things I didn't mess up today, either, so I guess I had a good day, too. I was just thinking about you and missing you, so I thought I'd call."

A few minutes later they said good night, gave hugs and kisses over the phone, and hung up.

After Lisa turned off the light that night, she fell into a peaceful sleep, without thinking any more about the blank application on her desk.

"BOMBS AWAY!" ALEX howled outside Stevie's bedroom door. She heard a pillow hit the door but had almost no trouble ignoring it. She'd slid her desk chair under the doorknob and muffled the outside noise by piling all the pillows from her bed, chair, and window seat around the door. Her brothers could feel free to reenact all of World War II right outside her room. She intended to enjoy some peace and quiet.

She went to her closet. Carole had once remarked that it took considerable courage every time Stevie opened her closet door, and Stevie summoned that courage now. Her closet tended to be the repository of everything her mother told her to pick up, plus laundry, clean and dirty.

Stevie knew exactly what she was looking for and exactly where it was. It was the large shoe box on top of her laundry—the clean pile.

She opened the door a crack and a few things tumbled out. She shoved them back in and reached around until her hand found the item she was seeking. She grasped it firmly and brought the box out into her room, shoving the door closed behind her with her hip.

She carried the box to her comfortable chair and sat down, hardly noticing that it wasn't so comfortable without any pillows. Her focus was total. She opened the box. There they were: the most beautiful dress boots she'd ever owned.

Her hands slid over the glossy leather, pausing at the small shiny buckle. Most tall riding boots were black, and that was fine most of the time. This time, however, Stevie had chosen a rich mahogany brown that seemed to her the most beautiful color in the world.

She removed the cardboard pieces that held the tops firm and reached down into the toes to take out the crumpled paper. She pulled on the left boot first, reveling in the ease with which it slid over her ankle and up her calf. It wasn't loose, but it wasn't tight, either. It was perfect.

She stood and walked to the mirror, just as she'd done at the tack shop, hoping that the boot would look as wonderful now as it did then. It looked better. She grinned, then hobbled back to put on the other boot.

The pair together looked even better than the one alone had looked. She wiggled her toes. There was plenty of room.

Luscious was the word that came to mind. She sighed with contentment, instantly seeing herself in a riding ring, surrounded by an adoring audience and an admiring panel of judges. With boots like these, nobody would ever ride the dressage course backward. It would be impossible to make a mistake dressed in these.

She wiggled her ankles. The boots were a little stiff, but new boots were supposed to be a little stiff. She'd have to wear them—and wear them often—to break them in for competition.

Suddenly she didn't feel so good. She had bought the boots with the last of the money she had. She couldn't go to the CI without boots, and now that she had boots, she didn't know how she was going to pay for the CI.

She sat down and took off the boots. Carefully, she put them back in the box, feeling how smooth and supple they were and enjoying the spicy scent of fresh leather. She put the top on the box and put the boots back in her closet.

She fetched a couple of the pillows from her door and retreated to her bed, where her history textbook awaited her attention. It didn't get her attention. Once the boots were back in her closet, the only thing she could think of was money. She didn't have any.

Not only had she spent all her money on the boots, she'd spent everything she had been counting on for Christmas

51

presents for her friends and family, too. The only present she'd paid for was the photograph for her parents. She had six dollars left for everything else.

The phone rang. Stevie picked it up, and Carole started right in.

"I've been thinking about something," she said.

"And it is?"

"Well, since there's so much going on, like finishing up projects in school"—Stevie knew Carole was having trouble with the science project—"and Christmas, and getting ready for the CI, and the Starlight Ride and everything . . ." She paused and took a breath. Stevie waited. "Well, what would you think if we, I mean the three of us, waited until after Christmas to exchange presents? We could have our own Christmas at the stable before we go to the CI."

"Christmas in a stable? Sounds kind of traditional to me," Stevie joked.

"No, really, I mean it," said Carole.

Stevie thought about it for a second. There was a lot to be said for the idea. Even if she couldn't figure out how to pay for the CI, there was no way she'd miss the night at the stable with her friends, and she'd have a whole day after Christmas, maybe with a couple of fat Christmas checks in hand, to find nice presents for her friends.

"I think I like it," she said.

"I bet Lisa will, too," said Carole.

Stevie looked at her clock. It was too late to call Lisa that night.

"I'll see her in the morning on the way to school, probably," Stevie said, expecting she'd miss the bus, as usual. "I'll ask her about it then."

"Good idea. And if you miss her, I'll catch her after the assembly at school."

"Deal," said Stevie. They said good night and hung up.

Stevie glanced at her history assignment and, having decided she knew enough to get by in class, turned out her light.

Sleep didn't come easily, though. She worried for a few minutes about how she would pay for the CI, but she found herself worrying even more about how Carole would manage it. Carole was such a great rider, and Starlight was such an inspired jumper. They *had* to go.

If she could give any present in the world to Carole, she would make it possible for her to go to the CI, but Carole couldn't even tell Stevie about her problem. How could Stevie help someone who wouldn't ask her for help? And how could she help someone else when she couldn't do a darn thing for herself?

6

"OH, STEVIE! THEY'RE beautiful!" Lisa said, admiring the new boots as Stevie took them out of the box. The girls were in the locker area at Pine Hollow, getting ready for class. "And you're going to wear them for just us, here at the stable in a class?"

Stevie ran her hand along the smooth leather before inserting her boot hooks and pulling the first boot up her left calf. "Just for you," she said. "Well, not really. I've got to break them in. They're a bit stiff, and they'll need to be comfortable before I can wear them in a competition."

Lisa handed her the second boot and Stevie repeated the operation.

"Wow," said Carole, entering the locker area just as

54

Stevie stood up. "Lisa told me you got new boots, but nothing she said led me to believe they were that gorgeous."

Stevie smiled. She'd known her friends would be as pleased for her as she was for herself.

"On sale," she reminded them. She didn't have to remind herself, though, that *on sale* hadn't meant they were cheap.

Stevie stood up and wiped some imaginary lint off her britches. She wanted to look as perfect as she felt. She took a couple of steps. What she felt was stiff leather.

"Don't worry," Carole assured her. "With that kind of quality, they'll break in easily."

"What's going to break?" Veronica asked, arriving late, as usual.

"Nothing," said Stevie, walking toward the stalls.

"Nice boots!" Veronica said.

Now, Stevie had bought those boots for herself, and having them, owning them, wearing them was a total pleasure to her. But even if she hadn't had that pleasure, every penny she'd spent on them would have been completely worth hearing the obvious envy that came from Veronica's mouth in those two little words.

"These old things?" Stevie asked, pirouetting around to face her admirer.

"Yes, those 'old things,' " Veronica said, realizing her

mistake. "But it's too bad they won't be put to any useful purpose—like winning blue ribbons."

"Don't be so sure," said Stevie.

"I am so sure," said Veronica. "I fully intend to take it all at the CI. There won't be one blue ribbon left for any of you." The smirk on her face was clearly intended to take back the admiration she'd been unable to control a moment before.

"We'll just see about that," said Stevie. It was a weak retort and she knew it, but considering her own doubts about even getting to the CI, much less competing and winning, it was the best she could do.

Lisa and Carole each linked an arm with her and the three of them headed to the stalls to make sure their horses were ready for their lesson.

It was a short lesson. The students had no sooner warmed up their horses to a trot than Mrs. Reg came into the ring and waved at her son.

"Storm's coming!" she said. "I just heard it on the radio. They've got a whiteout already in Cross County!"

"Uh-oh, work to be done!" said Max.

The weather didn't seem so bad to Stevie. It was cold outside; the thermometer had said it was just below freezing. But it wasn't snowing.

"Does that mean we'll have snow on the ground for the Starlight Ride?" Carole asked.

"Depends on whether it stays cold for the next week," Max said. "And at the moment, that's not what's on my mind. We've got to get busy."

"What can we do?" Lisa asked.

In no time at all Max put all the riders to work. One group was to bring extra grain into the stable from the grain shed. Another would put blankets on all the horses.

"It'll get cold in there. Out in the wild, horses grow shaggy coats in the winter, but we clip our horses, so we owe it to them to put their coats back on.

"The rest of you"—he looked right at The Saddle Club—"there are five horses out in the field, getting a little bit of fresh air. They've got to be brought in or they might get a whole lot more fresh air than they bargained for!"

"Oh, goody, a roundup!" Stevie said with childish glee. Then she remembered her new boots. She didn't want to get them soiled or wet with snow.

"Go put your paddock boots on," Lisa suggested.

"It'll look dumb," Stevie said.

"I don't think Nickel, Barq, and Comanche are going to care if you look dumb or not," Carole said sensibly.

Stevie handed her reins to Carole and dashed into the locker area to put on her old boots. Veronica was already there, changing into her street clothes.

"Aren't you going to help?" Stevie asked, then realized that was a silly question. Veronica never helped.

"I have to get home," she said. "My mother's taking me to the tack shop at the mall." Her eyes were on Stevie's boots.

"Last pair," Stevie said. "They're completely sold out." She felt wonderful delivering such bad news to Veronica.

"There are other tack shops," said Veronica.

Stevie stifled her giggle. "Good luck," she said without meaning it at all. She secured her paddock boots and hurried back to her friends, who were ready to ride.

The horses in the field seemed to sense the oncoming storm. They'd gathered in a makeshift herd.

"I swear they're waiting for us," Carole said, circling around behind the group.

"If they know it's going to snow, why don't they have the sense to come in by themselves?" Lisa asked.

"Because they know how much we like a roundup!" Stevie said. She rode to the far side of the group.

"Hee-ya!" Carole said, startling the group and getting the horses moving. Lisa and Stevie were positioned so that one of them was on each side. They began trotting systematically toward the fence, where Max was holding the gate wide open.

For a moment Nickel got an idea about heading into the

woods. Stevie convinced him of the error of his ways by chasing him down and getting him to rejoin his friends. It reminded her of the times she'd ridden out West at their friend Kate's dude ranch. The horse she rode there, Stewball, was a natural herder. Belle seemed to have some of the instincts for it, too. It made Stevie smile, but best of all, it made Nickel behave.

In a short time all the horses and ponies were contained in the schooling ring, and getting them inside didn't take a lot more effort after that.

The girls untacked their own horses, groomed and watered them, and gave each a tick of hay. Red brought each a blanket, which the girls secured.

"I feel like I should be reading Belle a bedtime story now," said Stevie.

"Well, it's dark enough outside," Carole observed. Stevie glanced out the window. She hadn't noticed before, but the sky had completely darkened, even though sunset was yet a while away, and snow was falling.

Stevie went to the big double door of the stable, which led to the schooling ring and the rest of the world. Lisa and Carole joined her. The flakes began to fall as they watched. As with many storms, the snow began slowly, a few flakes here and then some more. Most storms took a little while to work up to full blast, but not this one. The few flakes part was over within a minute; then the storm became a blizzard.

"The woods have disappeared!" Lisa said, amazed at the speed with which the storm had descended.

"That's nothing," said Carole. "The tree in the field over there is barely visible."

Stevie looked. It was really snowing hard. No matter how tired she was of all the snow that had already fallen this winter, the new snow descending on them so suddenly was beautiful and magical.

"It's so pretty," Lisa said.

"It always is when it's coming down," said Stevie. "But when it's been on the ground for a week and has gotten dirty, then it's ugly."

Max came over to them, and they helped him close the big doors.

"Your dad called, Carole. He said you should go to Stevie's and he'll pick you up there."

"Thanks," said Carole. "Is that okay with you?" she asked Stevie.

"It always is," Stevie told her.

"Now you all should get out of here before the snow gets any deeper," said Mrs. Reg. "I've got to start shoveling now—unless one of you wants to help me?"

"I think we'd better hurry," Stevie said. She knew Mrs.

Reg was teasing, but she also knew that if they dawdled, Mrs. Reg would find something for them to do.

They returned to the locker area to change into their street clothes. Stevie and Carole finished first and stepped outside while Lisa went to the bathroom to comb her hair. Someone had left something on the shelf in front of the bathroom mirror. It was a wallet.

Lisa picked it up and flipped it open. The three credit cards in it were sort of a giveaway, perhaps even more so than the designer label or the stamped gold initials V *di*A.

"Veronica?" she called out. But she knew that was a foolish thing to do. Veronica had fled the place at the first sign of work. She was probably well on her way to the mall by now. Lisa glanced into the money section of the wallet. She could hardly believe her eyes. Veronica had more than fifty dollars in there!

Lisa shook her head. It wasn't any of her business why Veronica had so much money. Nor was it any of her business where Veronica had gone.

There wasn't much question about what she was going to do. She picked up the wallet. Before she joined her friends, she went into the office and showed it to Mrs. Reg.

"I just wanted to tell you I found it, and I'll call Veronica and let her know. I also wanted you to see how much money there is in it, so, well . . ." Lisa got flustered. She

61

didn't like the idea that Veronica might accuse her of something, but she knew what was smart and what wasn't.

Mrs. Reg didn't seem to need any explanation. She took the money out, counted it carefully, jotted the amount down on a piece of paper, and handed the wallet back.

"Smart," Mrs. Reg said. "And you're being a good friend, too. Here, use my phone to call her."

Lisa checked the phone list that Mrs. Reg handed her and dialed Veronica's number. There was no answer. That seemed odd, since she knew Veronica had hurried to get home as soon as it was obvious that there was work to be done. And where was the housekeeper? Was it possible that in a moment of compassion Mrs. diAngelo had let the staff leave early just because there was a blizzard? Lisa guessed that must be the case. She left a message, explaining to Veronica that she had her wallet and she'd be home all evening if Veronica wanted to come and get it.

"You sure you don't want help with the shoveling?" Lisa asked before she left the office.

Mrs. Reg smiled. "No, I'm fine. You hurry home. Good night."

"Thanks. Bye," she said, and hurried to catch up with Stevie and Carole in the quickly darkening afternoon.

"What took you so long?" Carole asked Lisa.

She told her about Veronica's wallet.

"Boy, what I could do with that money!" Stevie said.

"Me too," agreed Carole.

"Me three," said Lisa. "Unfortunately it's not our money. It's hers."

"Do you always have to be right?" Stevie asked.

Lisa shrugged. She knew Stevie was just teasing. Stevie would no more take Veronica's money than she would flap her arms and fly.

Lisa pulled her scarf over her nose and shielded herself from the blast of snow with her backpack, and the three girls began their trek. Stevie and Carole waved good-bye to Lisa as she turned into her own driveway and approached the dark and silent house. Her mother was working late again.

As soon as Lisa got inside, she took Veronica's wallet out and looked at it again. It was a really nice wallet. She checked for phone messages in case Veronica had called while she was walking home with her friends. The light was blinking, but it was someone who wanted to put aluminum siding on their house.

Lisa picked up her backpack and the wallet and went up to her room. She had plenty of homework to keep her busy until her mother got home. And there was the phone call from Veronica to look forward to.

7

STEVIE AND CAROLE could hear the Lakes before they got to their house. Stevie's brothers had wasted no time taking advantage of the snow and were totally oblivious to its nearly blinding intensity. They were heaving snowballs at one another.

"Gotcha!"

"Did not!"

"Well, this one will!"

There was a brief moment of silence, followed by a "Yeooowww!" and then a "That one missed me, too."

"Right!"

Stevie and Carole ducked in the back door, dropped their bags off in the kitchen, and then sneaked back out through the garage entrance, where they found a pile of snow accumulating very quickly. In a matter of minutes they'd begun a stealthy attack from the rear on the battling brothers, who were only too happy to join forces against the girls.

"It's a good thing we keep in such good shape with our riding," Stevie said, packing a snowball tightly. She heaved it across the lawn and had the satisfaction of watching it hit her brother Chad on the shoulder. She laughed with joy, until Alex wreaked revenge with a direct hit to her rear end.

The battle ended as suddenly as it had begun when Mrs. Lake appeared at the kitchen door and yelled, "Cocoa!" A truce was declared instantly.

"You know, the only thing better than a good snowball fight is the cocoa afterward," Stevie told Carole, slinging her arm around her ally's shoulder.

"Weren't you complaining just the other day about all the snow we've had this winter?" Carole asked. She blew gently on her cocoa, waiting for the sweet concoction to cool down enough to drink.

"Yeah, but I didn't mean snowball fights," Stevie said. "I just meant I hate it when we have to ride indoors!"

Carole smiled. This was no time to explain that you can't have one without the other. She took a sip of her cocoa and listened to Chad talk about the fine points of lobbing snowballs until her father came to pick her up.

LISA TURNED ON another light. It was completely dark outside and the house seemed cold. She'd finished her homework. There wasn't much to do now that they were so close to the winter holiday, and it had all been easy.

She went into the kitchen and opened the refrigerator. Her mother had made a casserole the night before. Lisa took it out, turned the oven to what seemed to be a reasonable temperature, and slid the dish in. She looked at the clock. It was 6:30, so her mother would be home soon.

She walked to the window and looked out. The snow had stopped, leaving a few inches on the ground—enough to cover last week's snow, enough that her neighbor was sweeping his walkway, enough that there was going to be a snowman in the yard across the street, but not enough to close school or stop businesses.

She took out some placemats and silverware and began to set the kitchen table.

While she'd been doing her homework, she'd once again noticed the blank application for the show. She was going to have to do something about it. She could offer to pay some of the registration fee, but she knew she'd need her parents to pay most of it if she was going to be in the CI at all.

On one hand, it didn't seem like such a big deal. Her parents had paid for her to be in many shows in the past. But they hadn't been separated then, and they hadn't been talking about money being tight. It had just been an entry fee—no big deal at all. So why was it a big deal now?

Lisa took the nice napkins out of the linen drawer. She put crystal glasses on the table. Even though they were just eating a casserole in the kitchen, there was no law that said the table couldn't be pretty.

As soon as her mother got home . . . Well, as soon as she'd taken off her coat and sat down . . . Or maybe if they had a little visit in the living room after dinner—then she would ask. She only needed seventy-five dollars. Oh, and there would be some expenses once she got to the show, like food and stuff. She'd need a new hoof pick—no, she could borrow Stevie's. She'd definitely ask her mother tonight. How could she say no to something like that?

The kitchen door opened, and Mrs. Atwood came in. Lisa gave her a welcome-home hug. Her mother hugged her back, then smiled when she saw the table set and the casserole in the oven.

"But that's my best crystal!" she said, noticing the sparkling glasses.

"I thought they'd be pretty."

"And the linen napkins? They have to go to the laundry."

"I'll iron them," said Lisa. "I just wanted it to be nice."

Mrs. Atwood shrugged out of her coat and took off her boots.

"Thanks, honey," she said. "It is nice."

She looked tired. Even from across the room, Lisa could sense her mother's stress and fatigue.

"Long day?"

"Very," she said. "But the good news is that my boss gave me extra hours. I need to work all the time I can, you know."

"I know," said Lisa. She went to the refrigerator and took out the milk. Her mother picked up the day's mail and glanced through it.

"Oh, good," she said. "It's double coupon week at the supermarket."

Double coupon week had not always been a special occasion in the Atwood household. Lisa's heart sank. She'd been kidding herself about going to the CI, and she knew it.

Lisa answered the phone when it rang, because her mother was studying the coupons.

"It's Veronica," the voice on the other end said.

In spite of her low mood, Lisa almost laughed. Anybody else in the world would have delivered a greeting and some sort of pleasantry, like "hello." Veronica felt the need only to announce herself.

"Hi," Lisa returned.

"You've got my wallet?"

"Yes, because I thought you might want it tonight and nobody was going to be at Pine Hollow, so I brought it home."

"Well, I do need it," Veronica said.

"Then isn't it a good thing I brought it home with me?"

"I guess so," Veronica said. "Look, my mom and I are going back to the mall after dinner. I'll stop by your house and pick it up then. Okay?"

"Okay," said Lisa.

"You'll have it ready?"

"It's not going anywhere," Lisa assured her.

"See you later, then," said Veronica.

"You're welcome," Lisa said into the silent telephone. Veronica had already hung up.

After dinner, when the dishes were done, Lisa brought *Gone With the Wind* down to the living room to read. She turned on the reading light and settled into the sofa while her mother tried to balance her checkbook.

Lisa was startled by the sound of the doorbell. She had almost forgotten that Veronica was coming by. Her mother opened the door before Lisa could get to it.

"Oh, come in! How nice to see you! Would you like some after-dinner coffee? Perhaps a drink? Veronica, we haven't seen you here in a long time. Don't be a stranger!"

Lisa nearly gagged. Her mother simply couldn't resist being sweet to someone as socially prominent as Mrs. diAngelo, no matter how much Lisa told her she disliked Veronica.

The diAngelo women came into the living room. Lisa stood up and offered her hand to Veronica's mother, who paid as much attention to that as her daughter usually paid to anything Lisa ever did.

"You have my wallet?" Veronica asked with her usual grace.

"It's in my room," Lisa said.

Veronica tried, unsuccessfully, to mask her irritation that Lisa didn't have it waiting by the door.

"Why don't you girls go upstairs together for the wallet while we have a little visit down here," Mrs. Atwood suggested.

Veronica followed Lisa to her bedroom.

"You're on your way to the mall?" Lisa asked.

"Well, I've got to get a new pair of boots before the show," said Veronica. "I mean, my old ones have gotten marks all over them. I told Red to polish them for me, but he insists that they're scratches and they're not going to go

70

away. I can't compete in scratched-up boots! And then there's my jacket. It's from last year, you know. Styles change—even in riding clothes."

No, of course Veronica couldn't compete in scratched boots and an old jacket. Lisa understood that completely. It seemed bitterly unfair that she was worried about whether her parents might be able to help pay her entry fees while Veronica was busy outfitting herself with hundreds of dollars' worth of new clothes.

Lisa picked up the wallet from her desk. "Here," she said, handing it to Veronica.

Veronica took it and without hesitating did exactly what Lisa knew she would do: She opened it up to be sure all her cash was there.

"I had Mrs. Reg count it," Lisa said. "It's all there."

"Of course," said Veronica. She sat down at Lisa's desk while she slid the wallet into her purse. "But you never know who's going to be around at a public place like Pine Hollow."

Lisa did not dignify that with any response. She sat down on her bed and watched with amazement while Veronica shuffled idly through the papers on her desk—as if she were double-checking to be sure all the grades were As. They were.

Suddenly Veronica stopped. Lisa thought her face paled. "What's the matter?" she asked.

71

"Um," Veronica said.

Lisa stood up and walked over to where Veronica was frozen and apparently unable to speak.

Veronica had her hand on a sheet of paper on Lisa's desk. Lisa glanced to see what it was. It was the application for the CI.

"You sent yours in, didn't you?" Lisa asked.

"No, I didn't get it yet," said Veronica.

"Well, you sent away for it, didn't you?"

"Not yet," Veronica admitted.

This was bad news. "Veronica, the deadline is past," Lisa said. "The rules were pretty specific about that. You won't be allowed to apply now. Weren't you getting your father's secretary to do it for you?"

"She's been on vacation," Veronica said weakly. "She never got my message."

"Oh no," said Lisa. She wasn't really in the business of comforting Veronica diAngelo, but right at that moment, Veronica looked like she needed comforting.

"We've made our reservations and everything," Veronica said. "The plane, the hotel—everything."

"Look, I'm sure if you explain the situation," Lisa said. "Like call first thing in the morning . . ."

"They'll understand, I know," said Veronica. "I'll have Max call for me."

Lisa didn't think Max would be likely to do that and she told Veronica as much. "He's pretty big on individual responsibility," she said.

"Well, then, I'll have Daddy call," said Veronica.

Lisa wasn't sure that would work, either, but there was no point in telling her that.

"Or you could just give me a copy of this one," said Veronica, pointing to Lisa's application.

"No copies allowed," Lisa said, showing her where the form said that. "It has to be the original. They'd know if you sent in a copy."

"Well, it's a silly rule," said Veronica. "I'm sure they make exceptions every day, and I'm sure they'll make an exception for me. Don't you think so?"

Lisa didn't think so, but she saw no point in sharing her opinion with Veronica.

"I guess we'd better get going," said Veronica, standing up purposefully.

Lisa followed her downstairs and waved to her and Mrs. diAngelo as they left. Neither waved back.

She closed the door and clicked the latch, locking it for the night. Her mother was standing in the hallway.

"Odd woman," Lisa's mother said.

"And her daughter's no better," said Lisa.

Lisa reached out to give her mother a hug. Her mother

hugged her back. As the two of them stood there, Lisa realized that even though Veronica's wallet was filled with
credit cards and cash, she wouldn't trade anything to be in
Veronica's shoes. In fact, she'd rather be poor all her life
than behave like Veronica for one day.

"I CAN'T BELIEVE IT!" Stevie sputtered as she and Lisa walked to school together the next morning.

Lisa had sensed that Stevie was in a foul mood from the moment she saw her stomping toward her house. She hadn't wanted to ask, but now she felt a little trapped.

"What's the matter?" she offered.

"Look at this snow!" said Stevie. "A snowman here, a fort there, and it's still not enough to close school!"

"Didn't finish your homework, huh?" Lisa asked.

"I got most of it done," said Stevie.

"Don't worry," said Lisa. "You'll think of a good excuse by the time you get to school."

"Well, the worst part is that I was counting on having a

75

snow day to get to the mall to do some Christmas shopping."

"You don't have any money," Lisa reminded her.

"I've got a couple of dollars," she protested. "I could have gotten something."

"You should have gone with Veronica and her mother," Lisa said. "They were there after dinner. I know because she stopped by to pick up her wallet."

"What were they buying?" Stevie asked, not that she really cared.

"New boots and a new jacket. She wants to look perfect for the show."

"She's going to have to look pretty fantastic to overcome her questionable riding skills," Stevie said.

"Well, she never looks fantastic enough to overcome her questionable personality," Lisa said. "You wouldn't believe how rude she was. After she left, I took a vow of lifelong poverty so I'd never, ever, ever, ever behave the way she did."

"It doesn't have anything to do with money," Stevie said. "She'd be obnoxious if she were poor. You can have as much money as you want. There's no excuse for behaving the way she does."

"Do you mean to tell me that there are rich people who know how to say thank you?"

"Yes, I'm sure there are. They just aren't named diAngelo."

Lisa laughed. "That's comforting," she said. "Okay, I'll be rich then. And I'll say thank you."

They arrived at Fenton Hall and Stevie headed to the door. Lisa said good-bye and told her she'd see her that afternoon, but Stevie barely acknowledged her. Lisa knew Stevie wasn't trying to be rude. She was trying to decide how to explain the absence of homework to a couple of her teachers.

Lisa hurried on to her own school, relieved that she didn't have to do the same.

LISA WAS THE first of The Saddle Club to get to the stable that afternoon. Although she was looking forward to seeing her friends, she was glad for a little bit of quiet time to spend with Prancer. She had some decisions to make, and she had the feeling they would be easier if she talked them over with Prancer than with Carole and Stevie.

She went to pick up her grooming bucket in the tack room, but as she passed Max's office, she couldn't help hearing the loud voices coming from inside. Actually there was only one loud voice, and it was Veronica's. The door was closed. She couldn't hear what this afternoon's tantrum was about, but she could sure tell it was a tantrum. Max spoke softly, but in his firm instructor's voice, in response to Veronica's rants. In spite of her curiosity, Lisa didn't want to eavesdrop. Veronica's tantrums were rarely worth listening to.

She picked up her bucket and went straight to Prancer's stall.

The mare lifted her head alertly when Lisa arrived, anticipating a nice grooming. Lisa patted her cheek in the special way that Prancer loved and reached into her pocket for the carrot she'd saved from lunch. Prancer lipped it out of her palm and chomped contentedly.

Lisa took out a brush and began the grooming.

She'd barely finished one side with the brush when she became aware that Veronica was standing outside the stall, watching.

Stevie would have said something smart, like telling Veronica that the activity was called grooming and that people who cared about horses did it. Lisa wasn't as good as Stevie at saying things like that. They never sounded right coming out of her mouth.

"How was your shopping trip last night?" Lisa asked.

"A disaster," said Veronica. She made a terrible face to emphasize the awfulness of it.

Lisa thought that maybe the mall had been especially crowded or something. She waited for clarification. It came.

"They didn't have any decent boots," Veronica said.

"Oh."

"But that's not why I'm here," she said.

At least she was getting to the point.

"I had my father call the CI administrators today—like his secretary should have done last week. They refused to send the application. They had the gall to say we'd missed the deadline. I can apply again next year—if I apply on time. Can you believe it?"

Lisa could believe it. That's what the rules said. A competition was entitled to establish whatever rules it wanted, and almost all competitions had some sort of deadline.

"This woman told my father—like she didn't know whom she was speaking to—that it's an invitational. Only so many invitations were sent out and that's that. She said I can't use a copy."

"Oh, I'm sorry about that, Veronica. That's too bad."

Lisa wasn't in a mood to gloat, but she was tempted. She could just imagine Mr. diAngelo trying to throw his weight around.

Veronica continued. "Well, the woman there did say that it's the application form that's important, not the person who requested it."

"What?"

"She told Daddy that if somebody else has a form they aren't using, I can submit that—as long as it gets in on time."

"Oh," said Lisa. She had the feeling that Veronica was about to get to the point. She also had the feeling it was going to be pretty uncomfortable. She was right.

"So you have to give me your form."

It was beginning to sink in. Veronica had seen that Lisa's form was still blank and, therefore, something Veronica could use.

"You expect me to just give it to you?" she asked. "What makes you think I'd do that?"

"Well," Veronica began, "the whole thing is about Pine Hollow. It's Pine Hollow that matters and how well Max's students represent him and the stable. The stable is far more important than any of the individual riders. Realistically, you don't have a chance of winning anything, you know. I mean, you're pretty good for a relatively new rider, and anybody here would say that, so I'm not just trying to butter you up, you know. But pretty good isn't going to be good enough at the Carolina Invitational. Danny and I are going to be great. Imagine how proud we'll all be when I bring home blue for Pine Hollow! Surely you wouldn't want to stand in the way of that kind of success for our very own stable, would you?"

Lisa swallowed and stared at Veronica, wondering if she'd really heard her right. She went back over Veronica's words in her head. Yep. She'd heard it right. And Veronica wasn't through yet.

"And besides, you can go to the show anyway. I know you want to be with your friends, and Max needs them to help transport the horses, so you'll have all the fun of being there and watching all the good riders compete. You can't imagine how much you'll learn just from doing that. It won't just be me that you watch. There will be a lot of other good riders, too. You'll learn a lot!"

Veronica's growing enthusiasm for Lisa's learning curve was beginning to get on Lisa's nerves.

"And just exactly what do you think I'll be doing at the show?" she asked.

"Well, I've given that some thought," Veronica said. "And I'd like to offer you the job of being my equipment manager for the show. You're pretty good at keeping saddles polished and that kind of thing. Max is always telling me about that. You could do that for me at the show. I'm sure you'd enjoy that. You always seem to like doing it here, right?"

"Veronica," Lisa said in her most controlled voice. "Go jump in a lake."

Veronica looked puzzled, clearly not understanding why Lisa wasn't excited about the opportunity she'd offered her.

"Is that a no?" Veronica asked.

"I think class is about to begin," Lisa said. "You ought to see to it that Red has Danny saddled up properly."

Veronica turned on her heels and walked off to find Red.

AS FAR AS Stevie was concerned, her entire day was pretty much a loss. First she'd had to go to school, and she wasn't at all sure her science teacher believed there had been a flood in her bedroom that had destroyed her lab report. The woman obviously had a suspicious mind, because she'd asked Stevie three times if her bedroom was on the second floor of the house. She wasn't having much more luck convincing Belle that she wanted her to change leads at the crossing point in the ring.

"Stevie!" Max said, exasperated.

"It's not me, it's Belle!" she said, knowing as the words came out of her mouth exactly what Max was going to say. At least she was right about that.

"There are no bad horses, just bad riders!"

"Yes sir," she said, and returned to the corner to try again.

Finally she finished the course and was relieved when it was Carole's turn for humiliation. She and Belle stood on the sidelines with the other riders. Unfortunately she ended up next to Veronica.

The last person she wanted to be anywhere near was

Veronica. It was the only possible way to take a bad day and make it worse. She'd heard Veronica whining in Max's office when she'd arrived. Veronica was hard to take even when she was in a good mood. There was no telling what could happen when she was feeling cranky.

Then something nice did happen. Veronica looked at Stevie's boots.

"Can't keep your eyes off them, can you?" she asked.

"You bought the last pair in that size," Veronica said accusingly.

"We wear the same size?" Stevie asked. She was a little surprised to have anything in common with Veronica.

"I could have gone to the mall last weekend," Veronica said. "And then I'd have them."

"Give me a break, Veronica," Stevie said.

"But I don't think I'd like them anyway. The heels are too high."

Stevie didn't say anything. It was all she could do to keep from whooping with laughter. If Veronica couldn't have something, it had to be bad. Even though she was having a rough day, the fact that Veronica envied her boots was almost enough to make up for it.

For the rest of the class, Veronica could barely keep her eyes off the boots, and Stevie felt like she was floating on air.

9

STEVIE ALWAYS SAID that her favorite part of Christmas was opening presents, but it wasn't really her favorite. Not that that was an easy choice. Christmas at the Lake household was always a wonderful day. Everyone woke up early and the kids got to open their stockings. When Stevie was little, she and her brothers were usually up before dawn. Now that they were older, they would stay in bed until a time their parents considered more reasonable, like seven o'clock.

This morning Michael had gotten up at six-thirty, but Stevie threatened to turn him to stone if she couldn't get more sleep. Seven o'clock was as late as she could hold him off. It was as late as she wanted to stay in bed, anyway.

Present opening happened after breakfast, and it was

always a spirited occasion. Then the Lakes telephoned distant relatives to thank them for their presents and catch up on news. This part was sometimes fun, depending on the relative and the gift that Stevie had to thank them for. Then came lunch, a casual meal for the Lakes on Christmas. And then came Stevie's favorite part.

It seemed to happen every Christmas. Her parents would get sort of droopy and tired and start talking about naps. Everyone would take their gifts to their rooms and play with them, try them on, or read them—depending on the present. It was a quiet time, perhaps the only quiet time of the whole year at Stevie's house. And one time a year, she loved it.

She settled onto her bed and thought about the busy days she'd had leading up to that afternoon. Pine Hollow had had its traditional Starlight Ride on Christmas Eve, and this year had been just as much fun as ever. The snow was still on the ground from the storm the week before, and that seemed to make everything glisten. The horses always loved the Starlight Ride, and the ride at night by torchlight was a very special time for the riders. There was always a bunch of people to welcome the Starlight Riders when they emerged from the woods and paraded to the park in the center of town. Everybody sang Christmas carols and Hanukkah songs and drank cocoa. And after the Starlight Ride, Stevie and her family had gone to the midnight service at church. It was always wonderful, especially the part when they lit candles and sang *Silent Night*. That was the one song Stevie always sang in tune.

Present opening had been good this year, too. Her parents loved the portrait of the four kids, and even Stevie thought it was a good picture of all of them. Somehow the photographer had managed to take a picture when Michael was not making faces at the camera. She wondered if professional photographers took classes on how to get kids to behave. It was probably a big trade secret, like how magicians saw people in half.

Her brothers had given her cool things. Chad had gotten her a CD and Alex had found a horse poster she really loved. Michael had made her a spoon rest. It was better than the ones she used to make, and she swore she'd keep it until she had her own apartment and needed it. He seemed pleased by that. Her parents had given her mostly clothes, and they were all nice. She was going to be well dressed for the rest of the school year.

Her brothers had liked the things she'd given them, too: a sci-fi book for Chad, a CD for Alex, and a baseball poster for Michael.

Only year or two earlier Stevie had discovered it was more important to her to give other people things they liked than to get things she liked. Christmas had taken on a whole new luster since then, and she felt especially good about this year.

Then she looked at the gifts she'd gotten from her relatives. Her New England relatives had sent her some fancy soap. An aunt and uncle in Delaware had sent her a copy of *Misty of Chincoteague*. It was sweet of them to remember her interest in horses, but Stevie had had a copy of *Misty* since she was seven years old, and she practically had it memorized. Another miss was the sweater her grandmother had sent her. It was angora, and Stevie didn't wear angora. It would look silly on her, and she couldn't even bring herself to try it on. The good news was that Granny Lake lived *very* far away and would never know. The better news was that Lisa was practically born to wear angora. Stevie made a note to remind herself to ask Lisa if she'd like it.

Stevie picked up the novel her parents had given her. It was a mystery by Dick Francis, who wrote about horses. She opened to the first chapter. By the end of the page, her mind was totally on horses, but not totally on the story.

The bad news of the day was that nobody, nobody at all, had given her money. She had absolutely no cash left and nothing at all to pay for the CI. There was no way she was going to be competing at that show, even if she owned the most beautiful boots in both the Carolinas. She'd hinted to her parents that there was one tiny thing more, but when they realized what she was hinting at, they'd said no. It felt bad, but Stevie knew it was fair. They paid for Belle's boarding and vet fees and Stevie's classes. Horse shows were extra and were up to her. What had happened to all that baby-sitting money?

Christmas and riding boots and ice cream sundaes at TD's.

That was it, then. She couldn't compete at the CI. She'd explain to Max and he'd understand. She knew Max would let her come along. In fact, he'd encourage her to be there because there would always be ways she could help out the other riders, but she'd be in the stands and not in the saddle when it came time to compete.

Maybe she couldn't show her stuff and give Belle the much-needed experience of riding in a show, but that was okay. She was pretty good at dressage, not great. In spite of how obnoxious Veronica always was, she was probably right that Stevie wasn't going to take home any ribbons. But the member of The Saddle Club who was just about guaranteed ribbons was Carole. Carole had to go. Carole had to win, both for herself and to beat Veronica in the jumping competitions. Carole could do it, and Stevie had to see to it that she got the chance.

"SEE? I TOLD you he never said it," Colonel Hanson said to Carole. He took a handful of popcorn from the bowl that rested on Carole's lap.

The two of them were sitting on the sofa in the TV room having a relaxing Christmas afternoon, doing what many other people were probably doing right then: watching the videos they'd given each other for Christmas.

Carole had given her father one of his all-time favorite movies, *Casablanca*. The question was whether Rick ever uttered the words, "Play it again, Sam." He didn't. They'd been through the piano scenes three times, and though he said, "Play it," he never said, "Play it again, Sam"—the words by which Humphrey Bogart had been known for so many years but which he had never spoken.

"It's still a great movie, honey," Carole's dad said.

"So let's just watch the rest of it," she said. "I love the 'hill of beans' part."

"Me too," he agreed. "Actually, I love every bit of it, and I guess that's why you gave it to me for Christmas—even though we already own it."

"We *owned* it," she corrected him. "It just got worn out from being watched so many times."

Carole and her father had a lot in common, including a passion for old movies, especially this one and the other one she'd given him for Christmas, *Citizen Kane*. She'd gotten them both on sale from the video store. Her father told her it was just about the best Christmas present he could have ever asked for, and she knew he meant it.

When the movie was over, Carole offered to take the popcorn bowl and the glasses to the kitchen.

"Only if you're going to refill them," said Colonel Hanson. "We've got a whole other movie to watch!"

"It's a good thing I could only afford two movies," Carole said, taking the empty bowl and glasses out. "Otherwise we'd be here all night."

"And what a night it would be!" he said, laughing.

When Carole returned, her father had rewound the first movie and was ready to start the second one.

"Good Christmas?" he asked.

"The best," she assured him. She tried to smile enough to convince him.

"Something's on your mind," he said. She never could fool him about anything.

"No, everything's fine," she said.

"I'm going to miss you when you go to that show," he said.

"I'll miss you, too."

"Wish I could be there to watch you," he said.

"Don't worry about it, Dad. You've watched me ride plenty of times."

"Do you really mean that? Because I've been thinking you were upset about something."

"I really mean it, Dad," she said. "Really."

Of course she meant it. There was no reason for him to be upset about not watching her compete, because she wasn't going to be able to compete and it was all her fault. If she'd saved more money in some kind of rainy-day fund—No, that was silly, it didn't take a rainy day for her to know that a bridle held together with duct tape needed to be replaced. She'd spent all the money she'd had, and now she couldn't do something she wanted to do.

It was going to be hard, though, watching her friends ride at the show and having to be on the sidelines. At least she'd be there for them.

"How was the Starlight Ride last night?" her father asked.

"Well, you were there," she reminded him.

"Just at the end. Not in the woodsy part of it. Tell me about it."

"It was great, Dad. Just like it always is. Only it was one of the best because of the snow on the ground."

"I saw you got partnered up with Veronica. Was that okay? I was a little afraid that would ruin it for you."

"Nothing could have ruined it for me. Besides, Veronica has decided she loves Starlight's new bridle, and it gives me great pleasure to have something she wishes she had."

"Doesn't she have a good bridle?"

"That old thing?" Carole asked sarcastically. "She's had it over a *year*. It's got scratches on it!"

Colonel Hanson laughed at Carole's imitation. "You're pretty funny, you know."

"It's easy to pick on Veronica," Carole told him. "The fact is, she's kind of sad. She has some good qualities—like she's a pretty good rider—but when she's trying to be the boss of the world and to show that she's number one in absolutely everything, she's a pain."

"That sounds very wise," said the colonel.

"Maybe it's the Christmas spirit," said Carole. "I'm haunted by it, like Scrooge."

"Speaking of which, why didn't you get me *that* movie, too?"

"Is that *your* imitation of Veronica?" she asked him.

He didn't answer. He just clicked the remote and the opening scenes of *Citizen Kane* began to flicker on the screen.

"Hand me the popcorn, woman!" he said.

She did, lobbing it at him kernel by kernel until he apologized.

By which time young Citizen Kane was belly flopping on his sled in the snows of Colorado.

CAROLE CHECKED HER list a final time. Everything was there.

"Okay, Dad," she said. "That's it. I've got everything."

Her father looked at the enormous pile next to her and said, "That's a good thing, honey, because I don't think there's anything left!"

"Don't be silly," she said. "We're going to be gone for five days. That's a lot of food and stuff we need."

"I've seen troops on maneuvers that had less stuff than you've got." He smiled and gave her a hug. "Have fun!"

"I will," she promised, hugging him back.

When Carole arrived at Pine Hollow, Stevie and Lisa helped her lug everything into the stable.

"Wow!" Lisa declared. "You've got more stuff than I do!"

Lisa was famous for traveling heavy. Her mother usually made her bring *everything*. One time she insisted that Lisa bring a hair dryer on a camping trip (Lisa had left the hair dryer in her locker, and her mother was none the wiser).

"Well, we need to have food for our overnight and for our trip," said Carole. "I'm sure we'll be able to get additional supplies when we get to the show grounds."

"Right," Stevie agreed. "I checked the Internet, and they do have supermarkets in South Carolina," she teased.

When they brought the last bag into the stable, Carole noticed that Stevie's pile wasn't much smaller than hers. Stevie even had two coolers, compared with Carole's single large one.

"Who's talking?" she asked.

Stevie shrugged. "I figured we'd need food, so I brought some."

"I think we'll be able to open a concession stand when we get there!" Lisa said.

"Good way to raise money," said Carole. She wished she hadn't said it. It was a subject she didn't want to touch on with her friends. "But we're going to be too busy, anyway. I'm so excited!"

"Me too," Lisa agreed. "And the horses are, too. I just

went to say hi to Prancer. She was stomping and snorting. She can't wait to get going."

"We're not leaving until the morning," Carole reminded her.

"I thought we might give the horses a chance to work out some kinks before they have to spend all that time in a van," Lisa said.

"Like a trail ride?" asked Stevie.

Carole nodded sagely. "Just what they need. They've been working long and hard at all that discipline stuff they—and we—are going to need for the show. This is a good chance to let them hang out."

"Us too," Stevie said.

Taking a trail ride was one of the things the girls loved best. It never took much to convince them it was a good idea. They stowed all their gear and food for the sleepover and the trip to South Carolina and had their horses tacked up in minutes.

As they left the stable, each, in turn, brushed her gloved hand over Pine Hollow's good-luck horseshoe. It was one of the stable's oldest and most hallowed traditions. Every rider touched the horseshoe before going out, even little kids on ponies with lead lines. No rider who had touched it had ever been seriously hurt. The shoe had been smoothed and shined by the touches of all the riders over the years. Some people thought the horseshoe actually had a magical quality. Carole suspected that it served as a reminder that riding could be dangerous and required attention to safety.

The girls closed the stable door behind them. Carole tugged her gloves up and her sleeves down. It seemed chillier than it had been when she'd been emptying her father's car. She could see her horse's breath. She could see her own. She shrugged. It was December. What did she expect?

The day before had been much warmer, and most of the snow from the last snowfall had melted. The ground was hard but firm, and the horses had an easy time crossing the field with the short-cropped grass. It was almost hard to remember how the field had looked in the spring and summer, filled with lush, green grass and surrounded by tall trees with big leaves.

And now it was getting dark, too, as it did so early in the December afternoons.

"We can't stay out long," Carole said.

"We'll just follow the same trail we took the other night," said Lisa. "The horses know the way, and so do we."

The trail was a very familiar. Even more important, the horses had considerable night vision. They'd be safe and Carole knew it.

Before the sun dipped down, they could see the stars

coming out, and then, as the sky darkened in the east, the moon appeared.

Stevie, in the lead, halted Belle when they came to an open space in the woods. She sat back on her saddle and looked skyward. "It's like . . ."

Carole could tell she was at a loss for words. "It's like our very own Starlight Ride," she said.

"Minus the other kids, minus the noise, and minus the cocoa," said Lisa.

"Don't be so sure about the cocoa part," said Stevie, giving the first hint of what goodies *her* coolers contained.

Starlight took a step backward and then settled into a comfortable pose. Carole shifted her weight in the saddle and rested. It was a perfect moment. She was in an utterly beautiful place with her two best friends and the three horses they loved the most. It was cold, the air was clear, the stars sparkled, and the bright moonlight cast shadows across the open field where they stood in silence.

As far as Carole was concerned, there was only one thing wrong: She had a secret. She hadn't told her friends that she was just along for the ride to the CI. She wouldn't be competing. It disappointed her a little, but at least she was going to be there and she knew she'd be helpful to her friends. There was always a lot to do at a show. She'd be able to do it all—all except one thing.

Starlight snorted. Belle shifted to her right.

"I think they want us to get moving," said Stevie.

"Lead on!" Lisa encouraged her.

The three of them urged their horses forward. Their goal was to get to their favorite place of all: the creek. In the summer they often lingered there, sitting on a rock and dangling their feet in the water. That wasn't going to happen tonight, but it didn't mean they couldn't go.

The creek wasn't much farther and the ride didn't take long. Once they'd satisfied themselves that their favorite spot was there and it would be there the next time they came, they turned around. A few minutes later, they were back in the same clearing.

"What's up?" Lisa asked, looking around.

It was as if the whole place had changed in the mere fifteen minutes it had taken them to go and return to it.

Carole looked around. Starlight sniffed. Everything seemed different and she didn't know why until she looked up. Clouds had moved in, obscuring the stars. The moon was a mere glimmer through the clouds, and it disappeared completely while she was watching.

"Weather's changing," said Carole.

"Tell me about it," Stevie agreed, reaching out to grab a snowflake.

"Really," said Lisa.

"I think we'd better get back," Carole told her friends.

The storm the week before had taught them that the weather could change quickly this winter, and that seemed to be what was happening now. They headed their horses back to the stable. By the time the girls got within a quarter mile of Pine Hollow, the big buildings had almost disappeared in the darkness and the falling snow. The horses, guided by instinct, took their riders back in safely.

"That was weird," said Stevie, dismounting.

Carole and Lisa agreed.

"But at least we're here."

"I hope the roads will be okay tomorrow," said Lisa.

"Oh, sure," said Stevie. "Remember how school was open the day after that last storm?"

It would have been hard for anyone to forget Stevie's tantrum about that.

"Why don't you let Carole and me take care of Belle while you make us each a mug of cocoa?" Lisa suggested. The deal was struck.

Lisa and Carole soon realized they weren't just taking care of Belle. They had to look after every horse in the stable. Max and Deborah had already left for the CI because of the classes he was teaching before the competition. Red was off duty, at home. Mrs. Reg was out for the evening. They were in charge.

They knew what to do based on their last snowstorm experience. First they made sure all the doors were snugly shut so that the barn would stay as warm as possible. Then they saw to it that each horse had a blanket.

They paused in their chores to have a cup of cocoa with Stevie, who then helped them finish up. Each horse got an extra ration of straw to keep him warm and an extra ration of hay to keep him busy and fed. It was plenty of work looking after one or two horses. It was almost overwhelming tending to thirty. But they shared the work, and by the time they were done, they were ready for their picnic dinner.

Outside they could hear the wind beginning to pick up, and sometimes it even seemed to moan. The stable's windows were frosted from the cold so that even the ones they knew were fairly clean (because they'd cleaned them only a few weeks earlier) were impossible to see through. Inside they could feel the cold. There was no doubt that the temperature was plunging. When they'd come in from their ride, they'd removed their jackets and were comfortable with sweaters over their shirts. By nine o'clock, their jackets were back on.

"I've never eaten with gloves on before," Lisa observed.

"Adversity builds character," Stevie said.

"That sounds like something you heard from a parent," Carole told her.

"Yep," Stevie said. "Every time I complain to my mother

about anything, that's what she says. By now I've got a lot of character, and I got almost all of it from my brothers!"

"I'll take another sandwich," said Lisa. She alternated eating with her right and left hands so that the empty one could hold the mug of hot cocoa. The girls were all grateful for the little microwave oven Mrs. Reg kept in her office.

By nine-thirty they were finished eating. All the horses had been checked and double-checked, all the doors were closed. The girls had used the dishes that Mrs. Reg kept near the microwave, and Carole volunteered to take their plates and glasses up to the house so that they could be washed, while Stevie and Lisa set up their sleeping bags in the hayloft.

Neither plan worked.

Carole zipped up her jacket, donned her woolly winter hat, circled her neck with her scarf, pulled on her gloves, and then picked up the plates for the short walk up the hill to the Regnery house. She opened the door. What greeted her was not the familiar stone path, nor even the stone path with a few inches of snow. The ground was under two feet of snow!

It wasn't that two feet had fallen already, but the snow had drifted up so high against the barn door that there was no way she could get out, and she could see that the drifts between the barn and the house were even deeper in some places. She looked at the plates in her hands. It didn't seem worth the trouble to fight the forces of nature just to avoid washing them in the bathroom sink.

She closed the door and retreated to the locker room, where she removed a few layers of clothing. It didn't take long to rinse the plates. She could get them up to the house in the morning; for now they were clean enough. She went to help her friends set up their beds for the night.

Carole ascended the ladder to the loft. "You know," she said, feeling a change in the air as she did, "if hot air rises, it's not doing much in here."

Although Pine Hollow's stable was pretty well built and snug, it wasn't built like a house. The walls were only one board thick, and above the loft where there were no horses to worry about, nobody had paid too much attention to filling in the chinks between the boards. Carole swore she could feel a gust of wind. She wished she'd put her gloves back on before she came up.

"It is kind of chilly," Lisa conceded, still admiring the work she'd done of laying out their sleeping bags and blankets.

"I can see the headlines now," Stevie said, pausing for dramatic effect. " 'Horse-loving Girls Found Frozen at Stable.' "

"I'm glad you got the 'horse-loving' part in," said Carole.

"I did that part for you," Stevie teased.

"Okay, so it's too cold for us to sleep here," said Lisa. "What do we do?"

"We sleep in Max's office," Carole said. "He's got a propane heater there, and as long as the propane lasts, we should be okay. In fact, I know where there's a backup canister, so we're definitely okay."

That seemed like a great idea until they lay down. With no basement or insulation under it, the floor was cold.

"Straw!" said Carole. "If it keeps the horses' feet warm, it'll warm us."

They started to wonder how they were going to explain the mess in Max's office but decided he'd understand, especially if Stevie did one of her super-special explanations.

The straw did help a bit, and it even made the floor softer for sleeping. The girls set the heater going, safely away from the straw, turned out the lights, and slid into their sleeping bags.

Carole left most of her outer clothes on but thanked heaven for her father's Marine Corps–issue down sleeping bag as she snuggled into it.

What an exhausting day and evening it had been. First there was all the planning, packing, and lugging, and then there was the trail ride and all the extra stable work.

"I can't believe how much we got done today," she said to her friends. But nobody answered: They were both sound asleep.

And Carole never got to tell them her news.

"OH, STOP IT!" Stevie said. Her brothers were all lined up outside her bedroom door, taking turns banging on it and then blowing in bone-chilling air. What a curse to have brothers like that!

They kept doing it, and Stevie got colder and colder. "I'm telling Mom!" she said.

"What?"

"Mom! I'm telling her. Dad, too!"

"Stevie, what's up?"

Stevie opened her eyes. She was in a sleeping bag on a layer of straw in Max's office. Her brothers were nowhere near. Carole and Lisa were sitting up on either side of her.

"What's going on?" Lisa asked.

"I'm freezing!" said Carole.

"Something's wrong," said Stevie, abandoning all thoughts of her brothers.

She stood up and flipped the light switch. Nothing happened.

"Electricity's out," she said, glancing to where she knew there was a digital clock. She was greeted by darkness.

The three girls stood up, looking at one another in the eerie light generated by the space heater.

"We'd better see what's going on," Lisa said. "If it's this cold in here, with the heater, something more than electricity has gone wrong."

She held her watch up to the glow of the heater and announced that it was 3:17.

Carole opened the door. As soon as she did, she regretted it and shut it again right away. The stable was much colder than the office was. The thought of cold horses made her open the door again, once she and her friends had put back on any clothes they'd taken off before they'd gone to sleep. What greeted them was bitter cold and fierce winds.

"The big doors are open!" Stevie said, looking around the corner.

Indeed, the wind had been so strong that it had managed

to stress the latch to the breaking point. Both large doors had flapped wide open and were allowing wind and snow into the stable.

"We've got to save the horses!" Carole declared. Lisa and Stevie knew she was right. These domestic animals were no match for nature's force that night.

The girls pulled their hats down on their heads and their scarves up on their faces. There was a lot of work to be done. The first job was to close the door and bar it shut.

"The doors won't budge!" Lisa said.

"Of course not," Stevie observed. "They're blocked by the snow."

It was true. The open doors had allowed the full force of the storm to enter the barn, and now they were completely blocked by more than a foot of snow. In fact, snow had filled the entire aisle of the stable. There was nowhere near enough warmth in Pine Hollow to melt any of it. An odd thing was that all the commotion of the wind and snow had set off the stable's emergency sensor lights, so the girls could see the mess clearly.

"What do we do?" Stevie asked.

"We shovel it," Lisa said logically.

"With what?"

"Manure shovels," Lisa said. She brought two of them

out of the tack room, handed one to Stevie, and kept the other for herself. She turned to Carole. "You look after the horses while we shovel. Make sure they're all right."

Carole returned to Mrs. Reg's office, where she knew she'd find a large flashlight, and began checking on the horses one by one, amused by Lisa's take-charge mood. She was glad for it, in fact. While there was no doubt who the horse expert was among them, Lisa's logic came in handy many times, and this was one of them.

There was a lot of work to do with the horses. Barq had worked his blanket loose and was shivering in the corner of his stall. Penny stretched her head out over the top of her stall, looking for comfort from Nickel. Carole put Penny in with him. The two ponies were best friends, and being together would give them a chance of sharing some warmth the way horses and ponies naturally did in the wild.

She did the same thing with Belle and Starlight, because they often spent time together and even now seemed happy to be together.

Danny was a problem. The high-strung gelding wasn't at all used to adversity—as if being owned by Veronica weren't enough adversity on its own, Carole thought. He was darting around in his stall, moving back and forth restlessly.

Carole reached in to soothe him. He pulled his head back and snorted.

"There, there, boy," she said, using her best horse-calming voice. He stomped on the floor and backed away, his ears flat against his head and the whites of his eyes visible. He was one frightened horse. "It's okay," she said. "Don't worry. At this rate, you won't be seeing Veronica for days. Is that good news or what?"

He raised his front legs in a little rear. That frightened Carole. It wasn't that she was afraid Danny would try to hurt her. She knew that wasn't what was on his mind. He was just panicking, and he was likely to strike out any way he could, rearing, bucking, and kicking. A horse who had lost reason could do real harm to himself, get caught in or scraped by something, even break a stall wall. She stepped back and thought. Whatever was going on in the horse's head, she wasn't helping. He'd been agitated before she began trying to help him. He was practically out of control now.

"Don't worry. I'm leaving," she said, backing up. Her mere movement away from him seemed to calm him a little bit. She still didn't like the way he looked or was behaving, but he was better than he had been. Maybe he'd calm down more once she and her friends got the snow out and the door closed. Maybe.

Carole went on to the other stalls, securing a blanket here, replenishing straw there. Then she looked at the metal water bucket in Peso's stall. It was frozen. There was a good inch of ice all around it.

If Peso's bucket was frozen, everybody else's must be, too. She'd never seen anything like that. She went and checked the thermometer that Max kept by the door of the stable. It was twelve degrees Fahrenheit outside. It couldn't be much more than that inside. No wonder the water was frozen.

Carole hurried to the faucet they used to fill buckets and turned the knob. Miraculously the water in the pipes hadn't frozen. She took an empty bucket and filled it. The only way to be sure the horses got the water they'd need would be to take buckets to them one at a time and let them have a drink. There was no guarantee that the barn would warm up enough to melt the ice before the next afternoon, and horses needed more water than that.

Thirty horses. Thirty buckets. She had her work cut out for her. Stevie and Lisa could help once they'd finished their job.

At the other end of the stable, the job that Lisa and Stevie had taken on was beginning to feel impossible.

"Every time I dump a shovelful out, three more come in the door!" Stevie declared.

109

Lisa agreed. The wind was blowing hard and the snow was coming down so fast that they were barely keeping up with it.

"Let's just do the part around the door," Lisa said. "If we try to remove everything from the stable, we'll never finish."

"And we'll freeze to death trying," Stevie added.

Lisa didn't want to tell her that that might actually be the case. It was better if Stevie thought she was joking.

"Right," she said. "So let's see if we can sort of sweep this stuff in the path of where the door swings—"

"Sweep! Good idea!" Stevie dropped her shovel and went back into the tack room, where she found a wide push broom.

"Perfect!" Lisa said. "Much better than these little shovels."

It was a much better tool and it made a big difference. They'd done enough shoveling that there were only four or five inches of snow, but it was cold and dry and moved readily with the broom. The job they could do was hardly enough to please a fussy housekeeper, but soon they had half the doorway cleared.

"Let's close this baby!" Stevie said.

The two of them got their shoulders into the job and were able to swing the big door shut. However, without the other door and a latch, there was no way to keep it closed.

Stevie leaned against the door to hold it in place and

scratched her head. Since there was so much padding from her woolly hat and scarf, the scratch wasn't getting through, and she wasn't getting any of her usual bright ideas.

Lisa held the push broom. She stepped back and looked at Stevie leaning up against the door, recalling how, so recently, they hadn't been able to budge the door an inch because of snow.

"Bingo!" Lisa declared. "Stay right there."

Stevie followed directions and didn't move. Lisa took the broom and began pushing the snow that blocked the other half of the door, only instead of moving it outside, she moved it to the inside of the now closed door—under Stevie's feet, around her ankles, all across the wide expanse of the door.

"If snow kept the door from closing, it ought to keep it from opening," Lisa said, admiring the foot-deep pile of snow she'd pushed against the door.

Stevie shifted her weight, releasing the door from her guard. It shifted toward her a bit, but then compressed the snowdrift that Lisa had created and stayed where it belonged.

Stevie took one of the shovels and helped pack the snow up against the door. Then, when Lisa had cleared enough of the drift from the other half, the two of them swung it shut as well. Lisa began piling more of the indoor snow up against the door.

"Nice job," Stevie said.

"But now it'll get warmer in here and the snow will melt. . . ."

Stevie figured out what she was driving at. This was temporary. They were going to have to do something else to keep the doors closed.

While Lisa finished her snowbank, Stevie opened the tool cabinet. She found a couple of sturdy boards, some hammers, and some nails. Until Max could replace the broken latch, they were going to have to make do with what she could find.

The two girls nailed four boards across the old doors and then strung fence wire from each of the hinges in a big X pattern, straddling the entire doorway.

"Genius," Stevie declared. "Pure genius."

Lisa clapped her on the back. "Yes, we are," she agreed. "Now let's help Carole."

They put the tools away and each found an empty bucket to use to finish watering the horses.

That was the easy part. Carole had saved Danny until last, and when the three girls returned to his stall, he was even more nervous than he had been before.

"I thought he'd get better when the wind stopped," Carole said.

"And it *is* a little warmer," said Lisa.

"Right, like it's zoomed up to maybe fourteen degrees in here," Stevie said.

"Well, none of that is making him feel better right now. I'm worried about what he might do," said Carole.

Stevie and Lisa watched the horse twitch, jump, rear, and buck. The ever-calm Chip in the stall next to him seemed to be catching it from him. He, too, was stomping.

"I think we have to tranq him," Carole said.

"How?" Stevie asked, wondering exactly how Carole figured she was going to give this high-strung, nervous, agitated horse a shot of tranquilizer.

"Very carefully," Carole said.

That did not make Stevie feel better.

Lisa and Stevie followed Carole into Mrs. Reg's office, where the medications were kept. Nobody ever liked to give a horse a tranquilizer, but sometimes it was necessary, and the girls had seen it done. They'd each given shots to their horses. It was something every owner needed to know how to do. It was also something they'd always done with the supervision of Max or Judy Barker, Pine Hollow's equine vet. But this time they were on their own.

Carole opened the medicine chest with the key she found in Mrs. Reg's desk.

"It's a good thing you know where everything is," said Stevie.

"Well, I've worked here. And I've been Judy's assistant sometimes, remember?"

"I remember," Stevie said. "And that memory comforts me greatly."

Carole played the flashlight through the cabinet, selecting a syringe and finding the bottle of medicine labeled TRAN-QUILIZER in Mrs. Reg's refrigerator. Expertly, she stuck the needle into the little bottle and drew out the proper dosage.

At least she hoped it was the proper dosage. Last time she'd done this for one of the ponies. Danny was bigger than a pony, but he wasn't a *lot* bigger than a pony. She was guessing. She knew it was a guess, and she hoped it was a smart one. She flicked her finger authoritatively at the syringe, brought the little bubble to the top, and pushed it out with the plunger.

"Well, that part's done. Here, you take the flashlight," she said, handing the light to Lisa.

Carole wasn't at all sure how she was going to convince Danny to let her give him a shot. But as they passed their food coolers, she got an idea.

"Don't we have some oatmeal cookies in there?" Carole asked.

"Are you kidding?" Stevie asked. "You're hungry now?"

"Not me," said Carole. "I just wonder if Danny wouldn't like a sweet snack."

"And who's going to hold it for him while he bites her hand off?"

That was a problem Carole hadn't considered, but she had an idea.

"Let's hand it to him on one of those shovels," she suggested. "They ought to be clean enough by now."

And so they did. Lisa put the cookie—and a piece of apple in case that seemed like a better idea to the horse—on the flat blade of one of the shovels she'd used to move snow. Carole went into Chip's stall and climbed up on the divider between Chip's and Danny's stalls. Stevie stood behind her to hold on in case she lost her balance.

"Okay. Now," Carole said, once she was in place.

Slowly and evenly, Lisa pushed the goody-laden shovel into the stall. Danny, cowering in the corner, didn't move. He shifted his glance back and forth between Lisa and Carole. Outside, the wind howled and a fresh burst of snow pummeled the wall behind him, startling him forward.

Lisa didn't move. She didn't even breathe. She held the shovel close to the wall of Chip's stall and waited, hoping to entice Danny into range of Carole and the syringe.

Carole watched from above, ready.

Danny's ears went back again. He stepped forward, snorting and then sniffing. Carole knew that when horses were frightened, their constitutions gave them two options: fight or flight. She didn't think eating an oatmeal cookie or an apple was really a third option, but it seemed worth a try.

The girls waited. The wind quieted for a moment, just long enough for Danny to let his guard down and for his smelling sense to tell him something good was being offered. He stepped over to the shovel, regarded Lisa suspiciously, and then leaned forward.

He chose the oatmeal cookie.

As he did, Carole reached forward ever so slightly and slipped the needle of the syringe into his neck. The oatmeal cookie was so distracting that he didn't seem to notice until she completed the injection and pulled the needle out again.

Then he got upset, and he was further irritated by another blast of wind against the barn. Startled, Carole lost her balance and slipped forward. Fortunately Stevie was on the job, too. She had a firm hold of Carole's belt and yanked her friend back. The two of them tumbled into the corner of Chip's stall, startling him.

"You okay?" Stevie asked.

"Fine," said Carole. "Never better, in fact."

Lisa came into the stall to look after her friends.

"What do you mean by that?" she asked.

116

"Well," Carole said, sticking the cover back on the needle. "I just realized how much fun it's going to be when we get to tell Veronica we had to drug her horse!"

That was going to guarantee each of them good memories for some time to come.

IS IT MORNING? Lisa wondered. She sat up in her sleeping bag and looked around.

It was definitely lighter outside, but the light didn't feel like daylight. It felt like filtered light, somehow very different from a regular morning.

Stevie was the lump in the sleeping bag next to hers. Lisa gave her a shake.

"I think it's time to wake up," she said.

That was when she looked at her watch. It was almost eight o'clock in the morning. They were supposed to have left at six-thirty!

"Carole?" she said.

Carole's sleeping bag was empty.

Lisa stood up and pulled on her boots. Stevie followed her example, not yet feeling awake enough to talk.

"Good morning, sleepyheads!" Carole said, carrying mugs of cocoa into Max's office. "Time for breakfast!"

"It's time to be on the road," Lisa said. "We should have left an hour and a half ago. Red's going to be annoyed and Max will be furious!"

"I don't think so," said Carole.

"Ye-es," said Lisa. "He's such a stickler for promptness and his friend is expecting us this afternoon and we'll never make it—"

" 'We'll never make it' is right," Carole said, cutting her off. "Look out the window."

Lisa walked to Max's window and saw why the light had seemed so odd. The window in the office was completely covered with snow.

"We're buried?" she asked.

"Not exactly," said Carole. "I've been exploring. The drifts are deeper on that side, but it's at least three feet all around the place, and the snow is still falling."

"You mean we've gotten three feet of snow in less than, say, eighteen hours?" Stevie asked.

"No," said Carole. "I checked the weather report on the

portable radio. Officially it's about twenty inches so far, but this place isn't called Pine *Hollow* for nothing. Lots of snow has drifted down here."

Then, like a dream remembered, Lisa recalled everything that had happened the night before: the struggle with the door and what they'd had to do to keep Veronica's horse safe.

"How's Danny this morning?" she asked.

"Still calm," Carole told her. "He's a little dazed, but he seems healthy: He ate some grain and let me pat him."

Lisa took her first sip of the cocoa, which turned out to be chocolate milk. "Still no electricity?" she asked.

"Yeah, and no phone service, either."

"Do you think a cell phone would work?"

"It might, if we had one," said Stevie.

"Mrs. Reg usually keeps an extra in her desk," Carole said.

"Well, then we have to call somebody who has phone service," said Stevie.

"Or a cell phone," Carole said.

The girls dug through Mrs. Reg's desk and found the cell phone. It had a very slight charge left. They crossed their fingers as Lisa dialed a cell phone number they all knew: Judy Barker's.

There was no answer, but she did have her voice mail on.

"This is Lisa Atwood at Pine Hollow," Lisa said, speaking

quickly before the phone's charge ran out. "I'm here in the stable with Stevie and Carole. We have this phone, but the battery's running out. Just want you to know that we're fine. We've got food for us and for the horses. If you can find a way to let people know—"

The phone beeped four times and then was clearly dead.

"I hope she gets the message," said Carole.

"I hope she passes it on," said Stevie.

"I wish Mrs. Reg had charged this thing," said Lisa.

"People know we're here," said Stevie. "Someone's bound to come get us."

"And until they do, you know what?" Carole asked.

"What?" Lisa answered.

"We're in heaven. I mean, all our lives, all we wanted was to be left totally alone to enjoy the company of horses, and now we've got it. Nobody to tell us when to do what. It's just us and horses."

"It's like Christmas all over again!" Stevie declared.

"Christmas!" said Lisa, clapping her hand on her mouth.

"What?" Carole asked.

"We forgot Christmas. We were going to do it last night," said Lisa.

"But we got too tired," Carole recalled.

"It's never too late for Christmas," said Stevie. "But I'm not sure—"

"Come on, let's get cleaned up and have a nice Christmas breakfast," Carole said.

Fortunately the heater was working and there was running water, both hot and cold, though the hot wasn't very hot. Lisa and Stevie freshened up while Carole assembled breakfast. Their coolers had protected their food from freezing. They had orange juice and bowls of cereal, plus breakfast bars and all the chocolate milk they could drink. It was almost like home.

They settled in the locker area, where there was a small table.

"Okay, who goes first?" Stevie asked.

Carole and Lisa glanced uncertainly at each another. Stevie shrugged. "Okay, I guess that means me. Not that it makes much difference now. But it's Christmas."

She reached into her bag and pulled out two things. One was a medium-sized package and the other was an envelope. She handed the package to Lisa and the envelope to Carole.

"Lisa, you go first," she said, looking at the package she'd given to her. "I hope it's okay with you, because I thought it was just about perfect for you and would never do for me. My grandmother sent it to me and I don't think she knows me very well, though I'm sure she loves me, but I couldn't see myself in it, and—"

"Oh, Stevie! It's beautiful!" Lisa said. "What a great color!" She ran her hands along the soft, fluffy bodice of the angora sweater. "Peach is my absolute favorite!"

"I thought it was," said Stevie. "I'm glad you like it."

"Like it? I love it! How can you give it up?"

Carole began laughing. Lisa looked at her quizzically. "Well, can you really see your friend Stevie, Ms. T-shirt and torn jeans, wearing angora?" Carole asked.

"No, I guess not," Lisa said. "All the better for me. And I'll even help you write Granny's thank-you letter."

"Oh, don't worry," Stevie said. "I spoke to her on the phone on Christmas. I told her it was beautiful and a great color. I even said, 'Peach is my absolute favorite!' because I knew that's exactly what you would have said."

"You're a great friend," said Lisa.

"Yeah, but the problem is that it almost guarantees me more angora next year."

"Pass it on, girl!" Lisa declared, giving Stevie a big hug.

Then Lisa looked at Carole and her envelope. "Your turn," she said. Carole slid a finger under the flap and took out a Christmas card.

When she opened the card, she found three twenty-dollar bills, a ten, and a five. The note said: "If only one of us can ride in the CI, it has to be you. Go for blue! Love, Stevie."

"Stevie!" Carole said. "How could you—Where did you—What?"

"Where'd you get the money?" Lisa asked, rephrasing Carole's stammering into the question Carole wanted to ask.

"My boots," said Stevie.

"But you needed those boots!" Carole said.

"They were beautiful!" Lisa told her.

"They still are beautiful," said Stevie. "But they weren't going to do me any good if I couldn't afford to ride, and I couldn't ride if I had the boots, so I sold them."

"To whom?" Carole asked, but then she knew. "Veronica," she said.

Stevie nodded. "It actually made me very happy to have something Veronica wanted so badly, and the only thing that made me happier was knowing you could beat her in all her classes. I probably could have beat her at dressage, but you're better than she is in everything. That seemed more than worth the trouble just to know that."

"But—"

"I know," Stevie said. "You're wondering what I'm doing here and what I intended to do at the show. Well, Veronica seemed determined to get someone to do her work, so I agreed to be her equipment manager. It was for the glory of Pine Hollow, you know. I didn't want her to embarrass Max by having a dirty saddle."

"Oh, Stevie!" Carole said. Her eyes were misty as she gave Stevie a hug.

"Okay, so enough about my presents," Stevie said. "Who's next?"

"I guess that would be me," said Carole. She reached into her bag and pulled out packages very similar to Stevie's, one medium one and one flat envelope.

She handed Stevie the medium one. "Aunt Joanna," she said. Stevie looked puzzled as she opened the soft package. "I didn't have any money for presents, either," Carole explained. "And then . . ."

Stevie finished tearing off the paper. It was a dark blue heathery pullover sweater with a turtleneck.

"I love it!" Stevie said.

"I hate turtlenecks," Carole told her. "And it was too big."

Stevie held it up to herself. Even wearing her winter jacket, she knew it would fit her perfectly. "The color is great for me."

"It matches all your jeans," Lisa said.

"Yeah, that, and this color hides stains. Do you want me to write to Aunt Joanna for you?"

"No, I already did it," said Carole, returning Stevie's hug. "Dad always makes me write a thank-you note before I open the next present."

Stevie shrugged out of her jacket and put the sweater on. It did fit perfectly. She put her jacket back on. "Sorry you can't see it. But I promise you you'll have many other opportunities in the near future. Now you open your present, Lisa."

"I don't know," Carole began protesting. "It seems sort of silly."

"No present from a friend is silly," said Lisa. She slid her finger under the flap of the envelope. Inside was a card, and inside the card was a fifty-dollar bill, a twenty, and a five.

"Carole?" Lisa asked.

"I knew you couldn't ask your parents for the show money, and I thought it was really important for you to go," she said. "It's the kind of experience that's super important for a relatively new rider, much more important than for either Stevie or me—in spite of Stevie's confidence in my ability to beat Veronica. And since I couldn't go, well, it had to be you."

"But if you had the money, you *could* go," Lisa said. "Why give it to me?"

"It was like Stevie and her boots," said Carole. "Only, it was my bridle that Veronica wanted. Remember that Danny's was over a year old or whatever it was she said about 'that ratty old thing'?"

"You sold her your bridle?" Lisa asked.

126

"For seventy-five dollars," Carole said.

"But then you couldn't ride in the show!" said Stevie.

"No, but I couldn't anyway. I thought one of us should and chose Lisa because of the experience it would give her."

"So what did you think you'd do while you were there? You were planning to go, weren't you?" Stevie asked.

"Sure. I couldn't let you guys look after the horses by yourselves. And somehow Veronica convinced me that I might possibly be useful to her as a coach while Max was busy with 'all those other kids.' That's the way she put it."

"You were going to work for Veronica?" Lisa asked.

"I personally thought of it as working for Danny, but you can put it any way you want."

"Oh, Carole!" Lisa said. "The way I put it is that you must be the best friend in the whole world to make such a sacrifice for me! Thank you!" She gave her a hug.

"Enough, enough!" Stevie said. "Let's have more presents! Lisa, it's your turn."

"Well, this may seem a little odd," Lisa began, trying to hide a smile on her face.

"Don't tell me you didn't bring any presents!" Stevie teased.

"No, I brought presents," Lisa assured her. "It's just that it's going to seem a little weird." She got up from the table and went to her bag. She took out one medium-sized package and one flat envelope. She handed the medium-sized package to Carole.

Lisa started giggling before Carole got the first piece of tape loose. Stevie suspected she knew the cause and began laughing as well. Lisa nodded at her, and that was enough to get Carole laughing before the sweater was revealed.

"A great-aunt," she said by way of explanation. "I don't even know her. I haven't seen her since I was a toddler, and she never sends me presents, but I guess she felt bad because of my parents' split, and someone told her I loved horses. So . . ."

Carole took off the last piece of tissue and held up the sweater. It was completely, totally, utterly covered with horses.

"I think they're stampeding," said Lisa.

"It's perfect!" said Carole.

Both Lisa and Stevie began laughing in earnest. There was almost nobody in the world who would wear that sweater except one Carole Hanson, who loved every horse that ever was, even knitted ones!

"I knew you'd like it!" Lisa said.

"Much better than I like turtlenecks," Carole said.

"And much better than I like angora," said Stevie.

"And better than I like knitted horses," said Lisa.

Carole removed her jacket and put on her new

sweater. It wasn't exactly ugly, though it was a touch garish. It really was a horse-lover's sweater, and as much as Lisa liked horses, the thing had practically been made for Carole.

"What a Christmas!" Carole said.

"What relatives we've got!" said Lisa.

"What's the other present?" asked Stevie. She held up the envelope.

"Um, well . . ." Lisa began. She couldn't finish the thought before Stevie had the envelope open. In it was a card from Lisa, and inside the card were seven ten-dollar bills and one five-dollar bill.

"Lisa?" Stevie asked. "What's this about?"

"Well, I figured that anyone with the most beautiful boots in the world should have a chance to whup the person with the biggest ego in the world at a difficult skill like dressage."

"But how'd you get the money?" Carole asked. "Your parents? You can't give Stevie the money they gave you."

"No, I couldn't ever work up the courage to ask them," Lisa said. "Though they might have said okay, and then I would have felt worse. That was what made me make the final decision."

"Which was?" Stevie asked, still holding the money in her hand.

"Well, it turned out that I also had something Veronica wanted."

"The application!" Carole said. "I was wondering where she got it."

"It was this big deal. Her parents had made all these plane and hotel reservations and she couldn't tell them she'd blown it. So she kept demanding that I give her the application. Finally I told her I would—for a price." She nodded at the bills in Stevie's hand. "Oh, and there was one other thing."

"You're supposed to be working for her, too?" Carole asked.

Lisa nodded. "Groom," she said. "That's my title. Or it was until the snow started falling."

Carole snorted with laughter. Stevie and Lisa joined in.

"Can you see her in the Four Seasons?" Stevie uttered while she shook with giggles.

"Wondering where we are?" Carole said.

"And there's nobody there?" Lisa added.

"No horse," said Carole.

"No bridle," Stevie said, laughing.

"No equipment manager, no coach, no groom!"

"And no money!" Stevie held up her cash triumphantly.

"Perfect," said Lisa.

"Absolutely," Stevie agreed. "We got the best of Veronica

just when she must have thought she'd gotten the best of all of us."

"Well, that, too," said Lisa. "But I meant that this seems like a perfect Christmas. We didn't all get what we wanted, like the chance to see our friends ride in the show, but we've each got a nice new sweater, and now we're going to have some time for nothing but horses!"

"Speaking of which," Carole said, "I think we'd better go give them breakfast and muck out some stalls."

There was always plenty of work to do in a stable.

13

THE SADDLE CLUB began by doing the unpleasant work—mucking out stalls—but there wasn't too much of it to do because there wasn't any place to take the manure. They made a small pile in the barn's only empty stall. There was plenty of fresh straw in the hayloft, and there was plenty of hay as well.

"I think I get what igloos are about," Lisa said, removing her jacket. "It's not exactly warm in here, but it's much warmer than it was."

"I guess the snow is some kind of insulator," Carole said. She'd shed her jacket earlier.

The combined effect of the small heater in Max's office, body heat, and the insulating snow had brought the temperature in the stable above freezing. The water in the buckets had thawed, and the horses seemed comfortable in their blankets. Although the snow was still falling, as much as the girls could tell by looking through the frost-covered windows, the strong winds had subsided. It was oddly peaceful.

Here and there a horse snorted, neighed, or nickered. A foot stomp on the right, a munch on the left.

"Sweetest sounds in the world," Carole said. She gave Barq a hug and a pat.

When the girls got to Danny's stall, he was totally cooperative, the complete opposite of the horse they'd contended with in the middle of the night. His ears flopped a little, and his eyes looked a bit glassy. "That's probably the remainder of the tranquilizer," Carole said. "I don't know how long it takes to wear off."

"At least he's in a good mood," Stevie said, patting him on the neck. He nuzzled his nose under her hair and tickled her neck. She giggled. "And I hope he stays in this good mood forever!"

"He's not a cranky horse," Lisa said. Some horses just always seemed to be in a bad mood. Danny was usually quite cooperative, though rarely as docile as he was now.

"No, I was just thinking how good it would be for Veronica to have an adoring horse."

133

"I think Veronica does enough adoring of herself without any help from her horse, thank you very much," Lisa said, recalling how warm and fuzzy Veronica had been about the favor Lisa had done with her wallet and how generous she'd been when she'd practically blackmailed all three of them into working for her at the show.

Carole and Stevie agreed with that.

"Look, we may not be bowing and scraping to Lady Veronica in South Carolina, but at least we can take care of her horse," Carole said. "Let's give him the grooming of his life."

"He's not going to be in a show," Stevie protested. "He doesn't have to look beautiful."

"No, but life was kind of tough on him last night," Carole said, recalling how they'd tricked him before drugging him. "I think he could use some positive attention. And it's a natural part of our Total Horse Day."

That was what they called it from then on. Everything they did was part of Total Horse Day. Once they'd finished grooming Danny, his ears were perked and his coat gleamed. They all, including Danny, found that quite satisfying.

Next they went through the stable, giving every horse at least a cursory grooming. When it came to their own, they did super grooming jobs.

Stevie looked to Carole for leadership when the grooming was done. "Next?" she asked.

"We ride," Carole said.

"But the snow . . . ," Lisa said.

"The indoor ring!" Carole said.

The door to the indoor ring was closed because there was no way to heat it, but if it was above freezing and they put on their jackets, they could ride as much as they wanted to—as much as their horses wanted to.

They tacked up.

"I think we should have a horse show!" said Stevie.

It seemed like a fine idea. The girls called it the Total Horse Day Invitational. There were three classes. First was the pleasure class.

"This *is* a pleasure!" Lisa declared as the three of them rode around the ring. At first they circled at a walk, and then they took turns changing gaits and directions. Lisa could feel Prancer's delight at being able to get out of her stall and move around. She hadn't been as frightened by the storm as Danny, but it must be unnerving for her to have all the sunlight blocked out by the snow. Lisa could feel Prancer's strong, supple body come to life in the ring and her strides stretching. Prancer pricked up her ears at the trot and shook her head. The bay's shiny black mane was lifted by the wind from her motion. Lisa took in a chestful of the cold winter air. Prancer did the same.

"Canter!" Stevie declared.

135

Prancer knew the word and responded immediately to Lisa's slight signal. Her mane lifted farther. Moving with the smooth rocking gait of this former racehorse, Lisa felt as if she were flying.

"Way to go, Lisa!" Carole called out.

But it wasn't really just Lisa who was going. It was Lisa and Prancer, moving as one, in complete unison as they circled the ring.

"Walk, and return to center," Stevie said, declaring the end of the show class.

"No doubt about who gets the blue here," said Carole. "Lisa, you and Prancer have never worked together better."

"It's the Total Horse Day experience," said Lisa, laughing. She felt good, too, because she knew Carole was right. And maybe it did have something to do with Total Horse Day.

Next was the dressage class. Naturally Stevie and Belle would excel at that. Lisa found the work tiring, complicated, and difficult. Prancer, still a relative newcomer at schooling, simply didn't have the discipline for it.

Lisa and Stevie had expected to register for the dressage class, but all three of them had practiced the routine. Carole went first.

Starlight seemed more cautious, more contained, than usual, as if the snow itself held his spirit but not his skills in check. He relied more on Carole than usual for signals.

Carole suspected he was distrusting his own instincts in the very unusual circumstances of the stable's being practically buried in snow.

It turned out that the very fact that he was less independent, more reliant on Carole's aids, and a little unsure made him do better on the dressage test than he had ever done before.

"Good job, Carole!" Lisa said, and Carole knew she was right.

"Not me, though," she said. "It was all Starlight."

"Maybe," Stevie said. "But I think you've been learning from my excellent example."

Carole laughed. "Was that Veronica I heard talking?" she teased.

"Perish the thought!" Stevie said. Then she amended her comment. "Obviously, you've been working very hard on your dressage techniques."

"Thank you," Carole said graciously.

Lisa went second and she did fine. She was working well with Prancer, though Prancer didn't seem to be in the mood for a highly structured exercise like dressage. Carole clapped when she was done, and Stevie did, too. Lisa was pleased. It had been a pretty good performance for both of them, at least better than usual.

Stevie went next, but her skills seemed to have slipped.

Or maybe Belle's had. Dressage was such a partnership between horse and rider that it was often difficult to determine where a problem lay when there was a problem. Stevie seemed to be doing everything right. Then Carole realized it was Belle. The horse was clearly edgy, uncomfortable in the cold, probably stressed by the storm. It was as hard for a horse to concentrate when she was stressed as it was for a person. Under the circumstances, Belle was doing pretty well.

"Nice, Stevie," Carole said when Stevie completed the exercise.

"I don't think so," Stevie said. "Belle's as nervous as a yearling. You'd think she'd never done a dressage test before, much less this one."

"I think she doesn't like snowstorms," Carole said. "Starlight's behaving a little strangely, too. Let's see how he does with jumping."

Setting up the jumps was a challenge, since most of the equipment was in the shed next to the schooling ring. They managed to find a couple of cavalletti and perched them on some benches that they pulled out of the gallery area of the ring. The result was two jumps about eighteen inches high, not a great challenge for any of the three of them or their horses. They decided that the course would involve going over each twice, from each direction. It would do.

Carole went first. Stevie watched, hoping to learn something, as she almost always did when she watched Carole and Starlight on a jump course. Watching them circle the ring in a warm-up before the first jump, Stevie thought Starlight looked tense. His muscles flexed uneasily as if this were all new to him, which it most certainly was not. Every time Carole shifted even slightly, the horse seemed to shiver in response. It was very unlike Starlight.

Starlight made it over all the jumps, but his movements were jerky and insecure. It was not a blue-ribbon performance.

Lisa and Prancer did better. Then Stevie circled Belle, hoping to loosen her up. She needn't have. Belle was already plenty loose, somehow super relaxed, which was part of the reason she hadn't performed very well at dressage. What had hampered her dressage performance aided her jumping. She responded gloriously to the freedom of cantering around the ring and soared over the jumps as if they weren't there at all. At first Stevie thought she and Belle were making the beginner mistake of overjumping— going too high over a low jump—but that wasn't the case. She and Belle were working together as if they'd been champion jumpers all their riding lives.

"Blue!" Carole decreed when Stevie and Belle came to a halt.

139

"No doubt!" Lisa greed. "That was really nice."

"Looks like a little snow changes our horses' personalities," Stevie said. "Belle was just great!"

"So were you," Carole told her.

"And it's not a little snow," Lisa reminded them. "It's a lot of snow."

Having finished their show, the girls took their horses back into their stalls and talked about the next event in Total Horse Day.

"Maybe we could do some driving," Lisa suggested.

"That ring's too small," said Carole, trying to imagine even the pony cart circling the indoor ring.

"But the rest of the horses and ponies seem jealous of the fact that Belle, Prancer, and Starlight have all had a ride," Lisa said. "We've got to do something with them."

"Then we should ride them," said Carole.

"All of them?" Lisa asked.

"Every single one," said Stevie.

So they did. It took them the rest of the morning and all afternoon, but every horse and pony got a little workout, and each of the girls got to ride ten horses until all thirty occupants of the stable had gotten some exercise in the indoor ring. Stevie admitted to feeling a little silly, sitting on the Shetland pony, Farthing, but Farthing was as worthy of a workout as any and didn't seem at all bothered that his rider was about twice the size of the five-year-olds who usually rode him.

Outside the snow finally ceased, leaving four-foot drifts all around the stable. Sound carried well across the snow-covered world, and even from inside the barn they could hear the sound of plowing on the nearby roads.

By late afternoon, when the last of the horses had been exercised, groomed, watered, and fed, the girls knew the sound was getting closer to them.

"I'm not sure I want this to end," Carole admitted.

"I might get a teeny-tiny bit bored with peanut butter and jelly sandwiches, if that's all we had for the rest of our lives," said Lisa.

"Not me," said Stevie, slathering super chunk onto another piece of bread. "As long as the milk holds out." She took a bite and smiled with satisfaction.

"Imagine eight hours of riding every day," said Lisa.

"I think I'm going to be a little sore tomorrow," Carole confessed.

"You?" Stevie asked.

"Even me," Carole confirmed. "That was a lot of riding."

"But it was good," said Stevie.

"It was the best," said Lisa.

"We should have a Total Horse Day at least once a year," Carole said.

"I'll order up the snow," Lisa promised.

"Yeah, but next time, there's just one thing," said Stevie.

"What's that?" Lisa asked.

"Make it on a school day," Stevie said plaintively.

Lisa laughed. Naturally Stevie would want that. "Pass the milk," she said. Stevie did.

There was a loud noise. The girls looked up. Nothing seemed to have changed. They were sitting in Max's office in the dim late afternoon light. Then they realized that something had hit the window.

They turned and looked at the window in time to see something else coming. It was a snowball.

"Who let my brothers come over here?" Stevie asked.

"Not me," said Carole. She went to the window. What she saw made her laugh. Lisa and Stevie joined her.

There, standing about ten yards away, on the hillside that led up to the house, was a person so totally wrapped in snow clothes—to say nothing of the fact that she was standing in three feet of snow—that she was almost unidentifiable except for the way she held her arms akimbo. Unmistakably that was Mrs. Reg, who often stood that way just before she reeled off a list of tasks that idle riders could start doing before they began collecting dust.

Carole waved to Mrs. Reg but realized the woman probably couldn't see through the steamy window. So she un-latched it and pushed it open.

"Girls?"

"Yes?" Carole called back.

"You okay?"

"Yes, Mrs. Reg," Stevie told her.

"We can't get through to you yet."

"We're fine," Lisa called.

"The plows'll be here in the morning."

"We're really fine," said Carole. "The horses are fine, too."

"Food?"

"Plenty for us," Lisa called back.

"And for the horses," Carole assured her.

"Warm enough?"

"Yep," said Stevie.

"Judy got word to me and your parents," Mrs. Reg said. "Thanks for letting her know."

"No problem," said Lisa.

"It's getting cold with the window open," Stevie said.

"Then close it!" said Mrs. Reg. She waved to the girls and then climbed back over the drifts, heading back to her house.

It was early, not yet six o'clock, but in midwinter that

meant it was completely dark: They didn't know how long the batteries would last on their flashlights. At least the horses were all cared for, and the girls had finished their own dinner, such as it was, and washed up. There was really not much else to do except go to sleep.

The three of them climbed into their sleeping bags.

"You know, we should have been sleeping in a barn somewhere in North Carolina tonight," said Carole. "On our way to the horse show."

"Where we would have been forced to do everything one Veronica diAngelo ordered us to do."

"I'd rather be here," Lisa said.

"Any day," said Stevie.

"Every day," Carole corrected her.

LISA WOKE UP to the sound of a plow. Carole stirred when she heard a shovel approach the door outside Max's office. Stevie woke up when her friends shook her.

"Stevie, they're coming for us!" Carole told her.

"We'll have a real breakfast," said Lisa. "No more peanut butter!"

She looked at her watch. It read 7:15. She couldn't believe they had all slept about twelve hours, until she remembered everything they'd done the day before.

"Oh, my aching back!" Stevie said, rolling over.

"Oh, my aching bottom!" Lisa declared.

"Oh, my!" was all that Carole said. Her friends laughed, knowing she didn't want to admit that anything to do with horses ever hurt but also knowing that it did.

The three of them climbed out of their sleeping bags and hurried to the window. They were quite unprepared for the sight that greeted them. There was a plow, there were four people with shovels, and there were six cars behind the plow: one belonging to each of their families (two for Lisa), a car from the local television station, and a car from a Washington newspaper.

"We're going to be in the news!" Stevie said.

Lisa began rolling up her sleeping bag. "Is there a photographer?" she asked.

"Two," Carole told her.

"Okay, then, it's time."

"For what?" Stevie asked.

"If we're going to have our pictures taken, we can at least be well dressed for the occasion. Does anybody have a nice new sweater to put on?"

14

THREE DAYS LATER everything had changed. A warm spell had hit Virginia and melted most of the snow.

"Does it seem possible that there was a four-foot drift there day before yesterday?" Lisa asked Stevie, pointing to the big double doors of the stable they'd fought so hard to close in the middle of the night.

"No, because I think it was a five-foot drift anyway," Stevie said. "But there's nothing like sixty-degree weather to change all that."

"Weird," said Lisa.

"Definitely," Carole agreed. "But the really good news is that Max said yes."

"He did?" said Stevie.

"To what?" asked Lisa.

"A trail ride."

"What a brilliant idea," Stevie said admiringly.

The three of them were tacked up and ready to go in just a few minutes, and their horses seemed as pleased with the notion as they were. They trotted contentedly across the open field that led to the woods. Nobody had to ask where they were going. As long as they could make it across the snowy patches, they were headed for the creek.

It turned out they couldn't make it that far. As soon as they reached the woods, they found snow that was too deep to be safe. They turned back, but instead of going into the barn, they rode to the crest of the hill across from the schooling ring. In the summertime it was their favorite place for a picnic between Pony Club meetings and afternoon riding classes. They couldn't exactly spread a blanket and chat, but they could sit in their saddles and enjoy the view. Besides, there was only a little bit of snow left on the hill, and it was easy on the horses to get up there.

"Did you see the news broadcast about us?" Stevie asked her friends.

"Dad taped it," said Lisa.

"Mine too," Carole told her.

"Actually, it was Chad who taped it at our house," Stevie said. "But that's because Dad couldn't figure out how to set the VCR. But he definitely clipped the news article. He sent it to everyone he knows, except Grandma."

"Why not her?" Lisa asked.

"Because you're wearing the sweater she gave me for Christmas," Stevie explained.

Lisa laughed. So did Carole.

"All that news stuff was fun," said Carole, recalling how the broadcaster had referred to them as "three spunky girls" and the newspaper called them "heroines of Pine Hollow." "But the best part was when Veronica got home."

"Ah, yes." Lisa sighed in contentment. "I don't think I've ever seen her so angry."

"Well, of course. She didn't get to compete, and we did!" Carole said, recalling their little horse show.

"I loved how she implied that we'd caused the snowstorm," said Stevie. "I mean, only Veronica could think that way."

"I gave her back her money," said Carole. "That should make her happy. I decided I'd rather keep the bridle."

"And I'm keeping my boots," said Stevie. "Actually, she told me she didn't want them anymore."

"I didn't take back the application, although, believe me, she tried to talk me into it," Lisa said. "So I've still got seventy-five dollars. What shall we do with it?"

"We?" Stevie asked. The money was definitely Lisa's and nobody else's.

"We," Lisa repeated. "We all earned it, we should all have fun with it, and I wouldn't have any fun at all unless the two of you were with me, anyway."

"That's the thing about friends," Carole said. "We look out for one another."

"Yes, we do," Lisa agreed.

Stevie smiled and nodded. They weren't ready to decide yet, but they knew they'd enjoy the money when they did decide, and they knew that the fact it had come from Veronica would make the choice all the more delicious.

They sat in their saddles in silence for a while, just looking down at the stable, now mired in the mud caused by melting snow.

"Looks different from up here," said Stevie. "Especially at this time of year."

"But it's really just the same," Carole observed. "That's what I like about it. It's always Pine Hollow. Our Pine Hollow. Whether we're stuck in it, riding around it, looking at it, it's just the same."

"Just like we are," said Lisa. "Best friends—the same as always."

"Best friends," echoed Stevie.

"Forever," Carole confirmed.

ABOUT THE AUTHOR

BONNIE BRYANT is the author of more than a hundred books about horses, including The Saddle Club series, The Saddle Club Super Editions, the Pony Tails series, and Pine Hollow, which follows the Saddle Club girls into their teens. She has also written novels and movie novelizations under her married name, B. B. Hiller.

Ms. Bryant began writing The Saddle Club in 1986. Although she had done some riding before that, she intensified her studies then and found herself learning right along with her characters Stevie, Carole, and Lisa. She claims that they are all much better riders than she is.

Ms. Bryant was born and raised in New York City. She still lives there, in Greenwich Village, with her two sons.